D1417740

DEVIL'S RIM

**Center Point
Large Print**

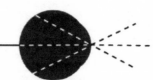

**This Large Print Book carries the
Seal of Approval of N.A.V.H.**

DEVIL'S RIM

Sam Brown

CENTER POINT PUBLISHING
THORNDIKE, MAINE

This Center Point Large Print edition
is published in the year 2010 by arrangement with
Bloomsbury USA.

The text of this Large Print edition is unabridged.
In other aspects, this book may vary
from the original edition.
Printed in the United States of America
on permanent paper.
Set in 16-point Times New Roman type.

ISBN: 978-1-60285-933-3

Library of Congress Cataloging-in-Publication Data

Brown, Sam, 1945–
  Devil's rim / Sam Brown.
     p. cm.
  ISBN 978-1-60285-933-3 (library binding : alk. paper)
  1. New Mexico—Fiction. 2. Large type books. I. Title.
  PS3552.R717D48 2010
  813´.54—dc22

                                    2010026748

CHAPTER 1

I WAS ON MY way to Mexico in the early summer of 1898, riding a good bay horse I called Drifter and leading an ignorant sorrel I called Feathers, partly because he was feather-legged but mostly because he was parrot-mouthed and birdbrained. You could've put his brains in a thimble. Actually, that's being a little too kind because the truth is, Feathers's brains would have rattled around inside a thimble like a pebble inside a tin can. But Feathers led good and was willing to carry on his back all of my worldly possessions—other than the clothes I was wearing and the saddle on Drifter's back. Of course, the rest of my worldly possessions amounted only to a couple of changes of clothes, an extra pair of boots, a few cooking utensils, and my bedroll.

I was in southeastern New Mexico Territory and the country I had been riding through for the past couple of hours was so sorry that a cow couldn't have found enough to eat to stay alive even if she grazed in a long lope. Nothing but rocks, alkali soil, prickly pear, and a few creosote bushes. The only living thing I'd seen in the last several miles had been a lizard standing in the shade of a creosote bush with his mouth gapped open in the heat. He acted like he'd just as soon let one of the horses step on him as leave the shade and let the ground fry his feet.

It wasn't long, though, before I came to the edge of a tall rim overlooking a basin. I pulled the horses up to let them blow while I rolled a cigarette and looked at the country below me. It was green down there, not lush green but at least cow-country green. And within the green, water in small lakes and creeks reflected the sun back toward the sky—blue sky except for the bank of thunderclouds building in the west end of the basin. A few miles out from the foot of the rim was a creek, wide and crooked and running the length of the basin. There were several flat-topped, rim-rocked mesas, the biggest being near the center of the basin, and scattered dark green patches of cottonwoods and cedars clustered along the creeks, springs, and seepy draws.

There was a town down there, too, built on the south side of the wide creek at the east end of the basin. Ranch roads led into the little town like cattle trails leading to a good watering hole, and there was a wide stage road coming into it from the east. There were also railroad tracks running north and south through the town.

I could also see the rooftops of ranch houses and camps scattered about the basin, and toward the east end I could see some farm fields, but they were few. The whole basin looked maybe thirty miles wide, and on the other side I could see another rim, rising blue in the distance.

It was all quite a contrast to what I had been riding through most of the afternoon, and in no way disappointing.

I snuffed the cigarette out on the swell of my saddle and soon found a trail that took me and the horses off the rim. My plan was to spend the night down there in that pretty little basin and to top out the next day on the blue rim on the south side, that much closer to Mexico.

The wide creek I'd seen from the rim was running only knee-deep to the horses, but it was boggy on the south side where we came up out of the water. Feathers bogged down to his belly and quit even trying to help himself out, so I dropped his lead rope and stayed after Drifter until we made it through. Then I hobbled Drifter and went back with my catch rope to get Feathers out. After a couple of gentle taps of doubled-rope persuasion on his worthless sorrel butt he decided he wasn't quite as ready to quit as he thought he was, and in a few minutes he was standing next to Drifter on solid ground.

By that time, the bank of thunderclouds I had seen building in the west was black and rumbling over the big mesa near the center of the basin. The wind was picking up, too, and the air was already feeling damp and cool.

Not long after leaving the creek I crossed a

wash and then came upon a fence with a gate no more than a hundred yards away. Soon after going through the gate, I crossed a dry, narrow wash lined with cottonwoods, cedars, and wild plums. I'd no more than come out of that when I came upon a ranch with a high-gabled, clapboard house painted white with red trim and a long porch across the front of it. There was also a barn, stack lot, windmill and storage tank, chicken house, springhouse, a set of horse pens, and set of working pens.

A woman at the corrals was struggling to hang a tall pole gate by herself in the wind. I rode up to her, stopped a respectable distance away, and said, "Ma'am?"

She jumped, and the gate fell with a rattle that spooked the horses and made them run backward. She wheeled around and looked at me. Then she shut her eyes from the blowing dust for a few seconds and pushed the hair out of her face.

I had my hands full trying to keep Feathers's lead rope out from underneath Drifter's tail. I finally got things squared away and spurred the snorting Drifter back up to the gate and the woman standing there. "Sorry, ma'am," I said. "Didn't mean to scare you . . . thought you saw me ridin' up. Here, let me give you a hand with that gate."

I got off, stood the gate up, and lifted the end

with the hinges on it a foot off the ground. "You want to pick that other end up?" I asked.

By the time the gate was hanging on its hinges, big drops of rain had begun splattering into the corral dust.

"You and your horses can stay in the barn tonight," the woman said abruptly as she turned and walked toward the house. "There's a cot in the tack room."

I took care of the horses—watered them and put them in separate stalls and fed them grain and hay. The tack room in the corner of the barn next to the wide front door had been turned into a bunk room of sorts, but it still smelled like a tack room— sweaty saddle blankets and horse linament. There was a little cookstove, an old beat-up metal bathtub, a washstand, and a cot, along with three saddleracks holding two saddles. Hanging on the wall were halters, bridles, chaps, spurs, stake and leg ropes, and catch ropes. On a wide shelf next to the door were brushes and curry combs, a bottle of Brown's Hoof Ointment, a small can of kerosene, gall salve, lump-jaw treatment, a bottle of Star-Crescent wire cut medicine, and a can of horse blister.

With just barely enough daylight left to see, I unrolled my bedroll on the cot, pulled off my boots, and lay down, listening to the barn doors bang in the wind and the rain hit the windowpane above my head.

• • •

Early the next morning, as I was tying my blankets onto Feathers's packsaddle, I looked up and saw the woman standing in the barn door, looking at me. She was holding a milk bucket in one hand and a cup in the other.

"Mornin'," I said.

"All that thunder and lightning—and no rain," she said in a voice that told me she was no true westerner. "It will be hot again today." She turned and looked outside, her form silhouetted against the gray light of dawn.

"Thanks for letting me have the use of the barn anyway," I told her.

She turned her head and looked at me again. "Are you looking for work?"

I thought a second and shrugged. "Depends."

"Too good to do some kinds of work, are you?"

I smiled. "Not too good—just too proud, I guess."

She let out a long breath. "I need a man who can do some riding for a few days."

"You the boss here?" I asked.

She walked into the barn and stopped three feet in front of me. She was about five-and-a-half feet tall and slender built, in her mid-thirties with brunette hair hanging limber and lifeless past a set of sagging shoulders. Her skin was tan and, although not leathery, showed the effects of the New Mexico wind and sun. A wrinkled cotton dress hung on her. The light in her hazel eyes was dim.

10

"Too proud to work for a woman, too?"

I smiled again and shrugged, and for lack of anything more intelligent to say, I said, "Depends," again.

She held out the cup she had been holding. I took it from her, saw that it was full of coffee, and took a sip.

"On what?" she asked, looking up at me.

I looked at her over the rim of the cup.

"What does it depend on—whether or not you'll work for a woman?"

I lowered the cup. "On the woman, I guess."

"Well . . ." she paused a moment ". . . I'm Judith Van."

I looked down at her again without saying anything.

She walked past me toward the milking shed at the back end of the barn.

"I'm Concho Smith," I said.

She stopped without turning around.

"I guess I can stay," I heard myself saying, "for a day or two."

She half-turned toward me. "The horses got out of the horse pasture. The fence needs to be ridden and the horses found and brought back."

I nodded and she turned and continued toward the milking shed.

Just past noon, I came back to the house, driving a small bunch of horses. Judith Van had the gate to the corrals open for me.

11

"Five head," I said as she closed the gate.

"There should be nine more—all branded with that same V on the left hip."

"I'll try to find 'em this afternoon." I glanced toward the house and saw a man sitting on the porch. "None of the calves I saw were branded."

She looked at me. "I'll bring a plate of food to the barn for you."

I unsaddled Drifter and laid my saddle next to the corral fence and spread the sweaty saddle blankets on top of it so they'd dry a little. Then I let Drifter get a long drink of water from the trough in front of the barn, curried some of the dried sweat from him, and fed him some oats in a stall.

By then, Judith Van was stepping inside the barn, carrying a plate of food. I took it from her and squatted down next to the stall door and started eating.

"Did you find out how they got out of the horse pasture?" she asked, standing in front of me, watching me eat.

"The gate on the south end was down . . . Guess I'll catch a horse out of the bunch I brought in to ride this afternoon."

"All right . . . Just leave your plate in the tack room when you're finished. I'll leave some towels and some coffee and a coffeepot for you."

"I'd appreciate the towels and the coffee," I said. "I got my own pot."

As soon as I was finished eating, I went back out to the corrals and looked at the horses I'd brought in. They were a pretty good-looking bunch, all geldings. Most of them had good muscle, bone, and heads, withers that would hold a saddle, and deep heart girths.

I shook out a loop in the rope I was carrying and flicked it over the head of a black with a star on his forehead and one white hind sock. He snorted when the rope drew up around his throatlatch, then walked toward me with his ears forward. He had been roped and led out before, which is more than you can say about a lot of horses on little outfits.

I looked in his mouth. A five-year-old.

The black took the bit but swelled up like a toad and snorted when I pulled the front cinch against his belly.

I turned him around, gathered the reins up, and eased into the saddle. He was tight as a fiddle string. I reined him all the way around to the left and then stepped him straight out. He clamped his tail, squealed a little, and hit a couple of crow-hopping jumps. I gathered him up and spun him to the left again, all the way around, twice. I was far past the stage in my life where I just dared something to blow up with me. If there was any way to talk a horse out of pitching, then that's what I wanted to do. When it came to riding pitching horses I was never any higher than somewhere in the middle of the cowboy clan. I'd much rather sit around with the boys and tell 'em about the bad ones I could ride or had ridden than actually do it. On the other hand, I wasn't going to let any horse buffalo me, either.

I spanked the black's butt with the ends of the bridle reins, called him a son of a bitch in my best bronc-peelin' voice, and told him that just acting like he was going to buck me off wasn't going to be enough for me. "You're gonna have to by-god show me!" I said.

He did.

He chinned the moon and kissed his butt, hit two hard, straight jumps that shortened my neck by a couple of inches, then sucked back underneath my left stirrup so fast he hung me out to dry like fresh wash.

I landed on my right shoulder, rolled over, and came up on my feet all in one motion, a little stunned that I had been planted in that barnyard dirt so easily. I watched him pitch toward the barn with my stirrups flopping over the saddle seat.

I glanced toward the house, and as luck would have it, there was a man sitting on the porch watching me. It's one of those immutable laws of nature—you fit ten good rides on ten bad horses and no one sees it, but the minute something gets out from underneath you, you can bet there'll be a witness to the whole sordid affair.

The black made a circle and pitched back to the corrals and stopped.

I caught him and cussed him again and made me a night latch with one of my piggin' strings run through the fork of my saddle and tied loose enough to get my hand around it. Then I tightened the cinch a little and stepped back on him, making sure my hand was in that night latch before I let him have any slack in the reins.

I gave him his head again and drove my spurs into his belly. Now, unlike before, I *was* daring him to pitch. I was mad now, and instead of trying to ease him around and talk him out of pitchin', I was just aching for him to blow up.

He did.

When I drove my spurs into his hide he squealed like a pig stuck underneath a gate and came apart again. Two hard jumps straight ahead just like before and then that same allemande left where he'd parted company with me. This time, though, I was ready for him. I had my left hand full of bridle reins, my right hand deep in that night latch, and I kept myself pulled up tight against the swells of my saddle.

I'm not easy to buck off like that, and I could tell that black hadn't had the kind of milk as a colt it took to stick my head in the dirt when I had that night latch closed.

"You counterfeit, farmer-minded son of a bitch," I said, getting my pride back. "I thought you wanted to pitch!" Then I pulled my spurs out of his belly and drove them into his shoulders. He hit two more pretty hard jumps, but I could tell his heart wasn't really in it anymore and that he'd had all the steel in his belly and shoulders that he wanted.

I let him pitch until he plumb quit, and then I spun him around to the left twice and back to the right.

He had some handle on him—not much, but some—and now he felt good underneath the saddle. His muscles were still bunched, but they felt more bunched for working and traveling than they did pitching.

When I got off and reset my saddle, I glanced toward the house again and saw the man still watching us. Then I got back on the black and trotted off to look for horses wearing a V on the left hip.

I found three more horses that afternoon and got back to the house with them about sundown. I grained all the horses, caught one for the next day, then turned the rest of them back into the horse pasture.

Judith Van had done what she said she would— there were towels and washcloths and coffee on the shelf between the gall salve and the wire-cut medicine. I carried the washbasin to the pump outside the barn door and filled it while the man sitting on the porch continued to watch me.

Back in the barn, I took off my shirt and was washing when Judith Van stepped into the doorway with a plate of food.

"Were three more all you could find?" she asked.

"So far," I said as I put my shirt on. "How long has it been since they've all been in the horse pasture?"

"I'm not sure. The ranch has about fifteen sections."

"All under fence?" I asked.

She nodded. "With one cross fence."

I took the plate of food from her and sat on the cot to eat. "Maybe I should ride the outside fence tomorrow," I said.

"All right," she said with little or no expression, just like she always did.

She leaned against the door and stared blankly into the barn. "It's hot," she said. "Maybe you can't sleep out here."

"I can move the cot out there where I can get some air if I have to," I said.

She nodded. "I've thought about putting a cot on the porch."

"Judith!" a man's voice from the direction of the house yelled.

She put the washcloth back on the shelf and took the empty plate from my hands.

"Thanks," I said.

CHAPTER 2

I WAS UP LONG before sunup the next morning. After graining the dun horse I'd kept up the night before, I boiled a pot of coffee, ate a can of cold tomatoes, then saddled up and got on the dun. He pitched a little but nothing like the black had done the day before, and in a few minutes I left to ride the outside fence.

The first small creek I came across was dry as a bone, but the water gap across it had been washed out from a rise in the creek god-knows-when, and horse and cattle tracks crossed it in both directions. I just looked at it and shook my head, remembering that it hadn't been that long ago when a man could ride from the Rio Grande to the Canadian border and not see a single fence—now they seemed to be nearly everywhere. I hobbled the dun and went to work, sweating and cussing and fighting gnats and deerflies, and thinking how much closer to Mexico I should have been instead of putting in a water gap on some little nester outfit.

That was the way that hot day went, with me finding one hole in the fence after another. A water gap out here. A few posts broken off and wire on the ground there. I saw good cattle—good Hereford cattle—but was in no mood to appreciate them, and the fact that none of the calves I'd seen had been worked or branded convinced me even more that the place was just another nester-run outfit with good cattle. The horses were kind of a mystery to me, though. It was as good a looking remuda as I could remember seeing, and not only that, the two horses that I'd been on—while still green—were pretty darn-well broke. At least, they were a lot better broke than what you'd expect on a fallen-down nester place run by a woman.

By the time the sun was sinking and it was time to quit for the day, I figured I'd covered no more than two miles, at the most, of that outside fence.

When I got back to the house and jingled the horses and caught one for the next morning the stars already lit the east. I was shaving when I saw Judith Van's haggard reflection in the little mirror on the wall. She was standing in the doorway, holding a plate of food. "Just put it on the cot," I said without turning around.

"You had a long day," she said as she set the plate down.

I didn't look at her. "You don't need a cowboy for a day or two, ma'am," I said. "You need a darn fencing crew—then maybe a cowboy could do you some good."

"The fence that bad?"

I lifted the razor from my face and turned and looked at her. She was leaning against the doorjamb. "It'll take me at least a week to get all the way around that fence," I said and turned back toward the mirror. Putting the razor to my face again, I began shaving around my mustache.

"And you have somewhere you need to be in a week?" she asked.

"I didn't hire on to fence . . . I'm on my way to Mexico." I wiped the shaving lather from my face with a towel and put my shirt back on before I sat on the edge of the cot and started eating.

"I see," she said. "Well—"

"JUDITH!" It was a man's voice coming from the direction of the house.

Judith stood up straight as a poker, like a soldier coming to attention. "I've got to go see about Sid," she said.

"Judith!"

She turned to go.

"I'll need some staples and wire," I heard myself saying. "I can't fix that mess of a fence without 'em."

She paused in the doorway. "I'll go to Chugwater tomorrow and get what you need."

"Thanks," I said. "For the supper, I mean."

For the next few days, I worked on that outside fence from daylight to near sundown. Every day I'd ride a different horse, and they were all at least a little broncy when I'd first untrack them—one, a solid bay, was more than a little broncy, and if it hadn't been for the night latch I kept tied through the fork of my saddle he might have planted me in front of the barn like the black had done—but you could turn them all around afterward and they would drop their heads and travel right without boogering from every little old rock and bush.

During that time, I would fix my own coffee and meager breakfast in the morning, take a can of peaches or tomatoes with me to eat at noon, and while I was jingling horses in the evenings Judith Van would leave a plate of food for me on the cot in the tack room.

Almost without fail the man would be sitting on the porch in the evening when I came in, watching me without saying a word while I did the chores.

One day while I was stapling wire to a post on a stretch of the north fence that crossed a sagebrush flat, I looked up and saw two riders coming toward me on the other side of the wire. When they stopped, the taller and older of the two, a man probably in his late thirties, pitched his horse some slack in the reins and said, "Didn't know Sid had 'im a fencer now."

I looked up at him and stretched my mustache into a grin. "Well," I said, "I guess, by god, he does."

"Not before he needed one—we're gettin' tired of pasturin' his goddamn cows," the puncher said.

"I imagine," I said as I held a staple in place over the wire and drove it into a post.

The other rider, probably in his early twenties,

twisted in his saddle and smiled, squinting against the glare of the afternoon sun. "So . . . how's ol' Sid and his mail-order bride gettin' along, anyway?"

"Wouldn't know much about that," I said. "Who do ya'll work for?"

"Bob Shiner—we just about surround Sid's little old place. We got a couple hundred thousand acres."

I looked at them for a few seconds, then smiled again and twisted my head like I was as impressed as it seemed he wanted me to be. "You seen any Van cows or horses?" I asked.

The older puncher leaned over and spit a stream of brown tobacco juice past the end of his stirrup, then said, "Why, hell yeah . . . They're scattered all over the goddamn country . . . Got four Van horses in the horse pasture at our camp right now. We'd a took 'em home but figured they'd just come right back, and we didn't want them across the fence from our horses and gettin' 'em cut up."

"The horse pasture at the Vans' will hold 'em now," I said. 'Maybe I ought to just come over there and get 'em."

"Suit yourself. It ain't far—a place called Clear Lake, about three miles north of here. There's a gate about a half mile up the fence."

"I'll just get on and trot up there," I said.

We rode the three miles to Clear Lake camp, gathered the horses in the horse pasture, and separated the three Van horses from the rest of them without talking.

"Much obliged," I said. "Name's Concho Smith."

"Well, Concho," the older one said, "I'm Malcolm Floyd and this is Billy Wright."

I leaned over in the saddle and shook their hands.

"I don't remember ever seeing you before," Billy Wright said. "You been in the basin long?"

"No, I was passin' through," I said, "and Mrs. Van let me hole up in her barn one night."

"And the next thing you knew you were buildin' fence, huh?" Floyd said.

"Yeah . . . ," I said. "Sorta like that."

"You ever cowboyed much?" Wright asked.

I grinned. "Oh . . . a little."

"Well, Shiner works a lot of men here on this place," he said. "You know, if you savvy cows just a little he might give you a job."

"I'll keep that in mind," I said.

Billy Wright laughed. "Shiner pays better and the Mex'can work is done by Mex'cans."

"I'd better get these horses started home," I said.

It was an hour past sundown when I got back to the Van ranch with the three horses from Clear Lake. When I closed the gate on them, I could see Judith Van stepping off the porch in the moonlight. She met me before I got to the barn.

"Where did you find them?" she asked.

"At a place called Clear Lake camp over at Shiner's," I said as I led my horse into the barn and lit the lantern hanging by the tack-room door. "One of the cowboys living there—Malcolm Floyd—said you have some cattle over there, too."

"Judith!"

She jerked her head toward the house and came to attention again.

"Mr. Van?" I asked.

"Yes . . . Sid," she answered, nodding her head.

"Why does he just sit on the porch?"

"A horse fell on him."

"He crippled?" I asked.

"Yes."

She started to say something, but before she could, the man on the porch hollered again, *"Judith!"*

"Your supper's on the cot—sorry it's cold," she said as she hurried out of the barn.

Three days later, I got back to the house a little earlier than usual and saw the man sitting on the porch again. After unsaddling and doing the chores I walked over to the house, went through the yard gate, and stepped up onto the porch. The man was sitting in a wooden chair with a pad on the seat. A pair of crutches was on one side of him and a Bible on the other. "Mr. Van?" I said and stuck out my hand. "Concho Smith."

Sid Van looked at me, then looked down at my hand for a few seconds; I didn't know what he was going to do. He finally extended his own hand.

The strength of Sid Van's grip surprised me. If his legs were crippled, his hands sure were not. For some reason I had him pictured as older and paler and frailer than he was. But he wasn't any of those things, other than maybe being a little pale. He was a pretty good-looking man. He looked like he was in his mid-forties. He had dark features and black hair, eyes that pierced you like a hawk's, and a strong chin.

After we shook hands he didn't say anything until I had a cigarette rolled and was lighting it with a match I'd struck on my spur. "How do you like working for a woman? I can't imagine it myself. Don't you have any pride?"

I blew out the smoke I'd drawn into my lungs and smiled. "She hasn't tried to do much bossin' yet. I just didn't know how much damn fencin' I was getting into when I told her I'd stay for a couple of days."

"How many horses have you found?" he asked.

"Twelve," I told him.

"Still two head short."

"Well," I said, "it's hard to build fence and prowl for lost horses at the same time."

"Just how bad is the fence?" he asked.

"Worse 'n a by-god," I told him. "How'd you let it get like that?"

"Damn!" Sid Van said, shooting those piercing black eyes at me. "Do you think it was in that kind of shape when I wasn't crippled?"

"Wouldn't know," I answered. "I wasn't around then. What happened to you?"

"A horse stepped in a gopher hole and rolled over on me when I was trying to head a cow."

"What does the doc say?" I asked as I snuffed the cigarette out on the sole of my boot.

"He don't know . . . And all I know is that I'm not any good to anybody like this. That horse would've done me a favor if he'd broke my neck and killed me outright."

"Horses are like that," I said.

"What does that mean?"

"I mean you can't ever trust 'em to do what you want 'em to do. If you'd *wanted* that horse to cripple you up like this he probably would have killed you."

"Well, hell! I didn't want either one! All I wanted was to head that cow of Shiner's . . . I spent my whole life putting this little place together, and now I can't even catch a horse and ride to the top of Big Butte Mesa and look at it."

"Which one's Big Butte?" I asked. "The one behind the house here a couple of miles?"

"Yeah . . . ," he said slowly. "I used to like to ride up there about sundown and get off and just sit there on the edge of the rim and . . . ."

Just then Judith opened the screen door, holding

Mishawaka-Penn-Harris Public Library

Title: The big lonely / Sam Brown.
ID: 33028003146190
Due: 12-21-12

Title: The crime of Coy Bell.
ID: 33028002997627
Due: 12-21-12

Title: Devil's rim / Sam Brown.
ID: 33028008449466
Due: 12-21-12

Total items: 3
11/30/2012 1:28 PM

Thank you for using the
3M SelfCheck™ System.
www.mphpl.org

a plate of food in her hands, which I took and set on the edge of the porch to eat.

"What do you think of that string of horses?" Sid asked after he watched me eat for a couple of minutes.

A coyote howled somewhere in the distance and a dove cooed from the cottonwoods by the dry creek just below the house. There wasn't enough wind to turn the windmill. "They're all right, I guess," I said.

"All right?" Sid said. "You must not know much about horses . . . and nearly all of 'em will watch a cow, too."

"Wouldn't know about that," I said. "All they've had a chance to watch when I've been on 'em is barbed wire and posts."

"What about that black?" Sid asked.

"What about 'im?" I asked back.

"He bucked your butt off, didn't he?"

"He sure did," I said. "Not that that'll get 'im many jewels in glory. He didn't ante up again when I got back on 'im though, did he." I handed the plate back to Judith, said, "Thank you, ma'am," stepped off the porch, and walked toward the barn.

CHAPTER 3

"THANK THE LORD . . . I finally got all the way 'round that darn fence today," I said to Judith a few days later when she brought my supper to the barn at sundown.

I'd moved my cot out into the barn where it would be cooler sleeping, and I sat down on the edge of it to eat. I looked up at her as I bit a biscuit and, for the first time since I'd been there, saw a small smile come across her lips. "And you hated every minute of it, too. Didn't you?"

"Every time I came to another place where the wire was down or a water gap was out I'd cuss and swear that as soon as I got back here that afternoon I was quittin' and rollin' my bed."

"Why didn't you?" she asked.

Now I smiled. "I was so tired when I'd get back in that I didn't want to do anything but eat and go to sleep. Besides, I hardly ever saw you. It's hard to quit if you don't ever see the boss, you know."

"So . . . I guess you'll be leaving now?"

I looked down at the food in my plate and sopped a piece of beef in brown gravy and thought of Mexico.

"I understand," she said. "You don't know how much I appreciate what you've done. You've been a big help to me. I don't want to keep you from your business any longer. It's been nice having someone here to talk to . . . not that we've talked that much, of course . . . but anyway, whether we talked in the evenings or not, your coming in was something I looked forward to, and wondering what you were finding or doing gave me something to occupy my mind with during the day. I don't know . . . it's hard to explain. I can get your money for you right now—I mean, if you want to leave this afternoon."

I put the piece of beef in my mouth and looked up at her again. "I'll tell you what I'll do," I said. "I'll try to find those other two horses before I leave. Since I've been workin' on that fence I haven't really had a chance to look, but I've been keeping my eyes open, and so far I haven't even seen any more fresh horse tracks. Maybe they're not on the place anymore—maybe they're on Shiner's, too."

Judith leaned back against the barn wall beside the cot. "Thank you," she said. "Sid wants you to go to town with us in the morning—it's up to you. Bob Shiner died in his sleep last night and they're burying him tomorrow morning. Sid wants you to help him get in and out of the wagon. It embarrasses him for people to see me helping him."

I thought a few seconds. "Okay . . . I guess," I said. "You sure know how to get the most from your help, don't you, lady."

She smiled again, a little bigger than the first

smile, and for the first time I saw the tiny dimples at the corners of her mouth. "There's a big gray horse we call Hank that we use to pull the buggy with."

"Your husband's pretty bitter, isn't he?"

"Very bitter," she said. "So, what are you, Concho—a drifter?"

I looked up at her again and handed her the empty plate. "Yeah . . . I was always going to find a good place and stay put but . . ." I shrugged. "I don't know. Life hardly ever turns out how we think it's going to."

"How well I know that," she said in a lonesome way. "You said you were on your way to Mexico—what's down there?"

"Don't know—haven't been yet," I said. "But I hear there's some good big ranches down there that Americans own . . . and cheap whiskey and señoritas—lots of 'em. And I hear they find a certain charm in old gringo cowboys."

Judith laughed quietly. The dim light in her hazel eyes seemed to grow a little brighter. "See you in the morning," she said as she stepped away from the barn wall. "I should warn you that Sid tends to get very irritable when he has to be helped."

Not long after Judith left the barn, I went to sleep, but after an hour or so I was awake again—awakened by the loneliness that men who sleep alone in bunkhouses and barns are familiar with, the kind that exaggerates the night sounds: the slow and steady pumping of a windmill, the scampering of a mouse along some old board, the night wind prowling through cottonwood leaves, the lonesome coo of a dove.

I got up and walked to the barn door and rolled and lit a cigarette. After I had smoked it and snuffed it out on the side of the barn, I looked toward the house and saw Judith in the moonlight. She was leaning against one of the support posts on the porch. The wind was blowing her hair and the long white gown she wore. The house was dark behind her.

The next morning I put the harness on the gray that Judith called Hank, hooked him to the open-topped buggy in the barn, then pulled the buggy to the yard gate and waited. In a few minutes, Sid and Judith came out the door and onto the porch. Sid was wearing a black suit and string tie and struggling along on his crutches. Judith was behind him, looking like I'd never seen her before. Instead of a drab cotton dress hanging loosely about her, she was wearing a black skirt and white blouse with ruffles at the collar and cuffs. She stood straight and proud. Her long hair had been put up on the top of her head with little strands of it falling out around the back of her neck.

I got down from the buggy seat and met them at the yard gate. "Good mornin'," I said.

"Well?" Sid said. "Are you going to help me get into the buggy or not?"

Sid's legs could pretty well hold him up once he got them both underneath him. The trouble, though, was he had a hard time getting them underneath him because he didn't have much control over them. In probably less than a minute I had helped him up and he was sitting in the buggy and his crutches were behind the seat.

The first two miles of the six-mile trip to town were covered in silence except for the rattle of the buggy and harness and the sound of Hank's black hooves on the hard-packed roadbed.

When Hank stopped and stretched out to empty his bladder, Sid said, "What's your given name, Smith?"

"Just Concho," I said.

"Strange name. Sounds more like a nickname to me."

"Well," I said, "it's the only one I got—guess it'll have to do."

"Where'd it come from?" he asked.

The gray pulled his legs back underneath him. "An orphanage in Texas," I said as I tapped Hank's rump with the lines and the buggy started on down the road.

"What's this town's name?" I asked as we entered it.

"Shinerville," Sid said sarcastically.

"Actually, it's Chugwater," Judith said.

It was a pretty little town, built right on the south bank of the creek. Cottonwoods lined every short street where houses stood, and shaded nearly every business on Main Street, the length of which we traveled getting to the Methodist church.

"Looks like everyone in town must be at the church," Judith said.

"Yeah," Sid agreed. "Everyone in the whole basin will be there. They don't have Bob's butt to kiss anymore, but they'll want to get in line to kiss Little Bob's butt."

"Is that why *we* came?" she asked.

"I came to pay my respects to Bob—you and Smith came because I told you to."

I pulled the gray to as quick a stop in the middle of Main Street as I could, and we stopped right in front of the Basin Bar, where two horses tied in front switched their long tails at the flies. The bar had a sign on the door announcing that it was closed for the funeral. "Let's get one thing straight, Sid," I said. "I came because Judith said you *wanted* me to—not because you told me to."

"Please, Concho . . . ," Judith said.

"Let's go!" Sid said.

I held the slack out of the reins.

Sid sat silent with his arms folded.

"Well, this is going to be just fine!" Judith said, folding her own arms in disgust. "I guess we can sit right here in front of the bar while everyone else is at the funeral."

"Okay—dammit!" Sid finally said. Then he said, slow and sarcastic, "Mister Smith . . . would you *mind* taking us to the church?"

I gave Hank some slack and smacked him.

"And I didn't come because you told me to, either," Judith said in a hushed tone when we were a half block from the church.

I stopped as close to the front door of the church as possible. "I'll help you get into the church and then I'll wait outside," I said.

When the church service was over we, along with just about everyone else who had packed the church, followed the hearse to the Chugwater Cemetery. It sat on a grassy knoll just back from the south bank of Chugwater Creek on the west side of town.

I stopped the buggy, got Sid's crutches, and helped him out.

Sid and Judith nodded to the people they stood beside at the grave, and a couple of men leaned over to shake Sid's hand. When the preacher was finished and we started back toward the buggy, Sid said he ought to go offer his condolences to Bob Shiner's son and pointed to a group of men standing off a little ways from the grave. "I guess we ought to go over there," he said.

When we were thirty feet from the group of men

a few heads began turning toward us, and the closer we got, the more heads turned. When we were six feet away a man stepped out from the group with his hand extended. "Hello, Sid," he said.

"Hello, Taylor," he said as they shook hands.

Most of the other men in the group stepped forward and shook hands with Sid and nodded and tipped their hats to Judith.

Then someone else said, "Hello, Sid," and the group of men parted. A man in his mid-thirties, about six-two and a little overweight, with slick hair, a frock coat, and five-dollar patent leather shoes, was looking at Sid and smiling.

"Hello, Little Bob," Sid said. "Sorry about your dad—if there's anything I can do . . ."

For a few seconds there was silence. A couple of the men looked off into the distance and a couple of others looked at the ground. Shiner's smile disappeared momentarily, then he said, "As a matter of fact there is, Sid—you could try keeping your stock on your place for a change. I'll be glad to loan you a couple of my Mex'cans to get that fence in shape, even though you're the one who insisted on building it to begin with."

"Done got it taken care of, Little Bob," Sid said with what was easy to tell was a great deal of satisfaction, "but thanks for the offer anyway. See you fellers."

After we were back in the buggy, Judith asked,

"Did that feel good, Sid—calling him 'Little Bob' in front of all those men?"

"Real good!" Sid said, then he grinned and added, "Almost as good as choking one of Bob Shiner's cows till her tongue lolls out. Everyone in the basin can call him Robert if they want to, but he was Little Bob before he went off to college, and he'll always be Little Bob to me. He never even spent enough time in the saddle when he was growing up to not be scared if a horse so much as wrung his tail. He still handles a rope like a ten-year-old kid and can't tell a springin' cow from a barren bitch."

"I wish you'd watch your language," Judith said.

"Well, he can't," Sid said, "and I told him that one time when we were arguing over a cow. I might not have liked old Bob Shiner all the time, but at least I had respect for him both as a cowman and a man. Bob earned everything he had—his land, his cattle, his respect. But Little Bob . . . he thinks that's all his by birthright alone. Well, the land and the cattle I guess are, him being the only heir, but he won't have my respect until he earns it. Little Bob running the Shiner ranch— what a train wreck that's going to be. At least maybe now people around here will have something to talk about besides poor old crippled Sid Van and his mail-order bride."

"Oh, Sid, please! For god's sake!" Judith said,

and from then on we traveled back to the ranch in silence except for the rattle of the harness and the sound of the gray's hooves on the roadbed.

When we got home, Sid and Judith went into the house and I went out to the barn. I ate a can of peaches and wrangled the horses out of the horse pasture again. Most of the Van ranch was too rocky for a horse to go unshod and not get sore-footed. The six head that I had been riding the most since I'd been there had all been shod, but two of them had already lost at least one shoe and the shoes on the other two were beginning to click, which meant they were loose and needed to be reset. The shoes on Drifter and Feathers—my own horses—needed to be reset, too. When it came time to head for Mexico again, I wanted them ready to travel.

I led the black and the dun Van horses to the big cottonwood tree just east of the barn where there was an anvil mounted on top of an old stump. I tied them both to a low-growing branch and started to work on the little dun.

In two hours I had the shoes reset on both the Van horses and turned them loose in the corral. Then I caught a sorrel Van horse and my own Drifter. Sweat was dripping from my face, so I got a drink of water from the pump in front of the barn and smoked a cigarette before I started to work on the sorrel.

I was nailing a shoe on the sorrel's left hind foot

when Judith came out of the house, carrying a pitcher of lemonade and two glasses on a round tray. I smiled when I looked up and saw her coming. She was still in her funeral clothes, but she had taken her hair down and brushed it out and she looked pretty.

I drove the last two nails into the sorrel's hoof, clinched them, and set the foot down. I stretched my back, took off my hat, wiped the sweat from my face with a shirtsleeve, put the hat back on, and reached for the glass Judith was holding out to me. "Thanks," I said and drank the glass dry before lowering it.

Judith refilled my glass from the pitcher, then sat down on the grass.

I sank down onto the grass myself and stretched out, looking up into the cottonwood above us. There wasn't even enough breeze to stir the leaves. "Hardest work in the world—shoein' horses," I said. "Either a horse is trying to jerk his foot away and kick you or else he's laying down on you."

"I'm sorry about the way Sid acted this morning, but I warned you."

"Yeah . . . well, don't worry about it," I said. "I can't say that I blame him."

"He started drinking as soon as we got home. I stayed out of his sight until he passed out."

"I expect I'd do that, too," I said. "I mean drink until I passed out."

"He just makes it harder on himself and everybody around him when he's like he was today—which is how he is most of the time."

"Makes it hard on you too, I guess," I said.

"Yes . . ." She started to say something else but instead stretched out on the grass with the pitcher of lemonade between us. We were silent for quite a while then before she said, "How did you happen to grow up in an orphanage?"

I didn't say anything.

"I'm sorry," Judith said. "I shouldn't have asked."

"Oh, it doesn't matter," I said, and it really didn't, it was just something I didn't talk about much. Most people, even those who had known me a long time, had no idea where I got my name.

"I was found wandering along the banks of the Concho River when I was about a year old," I said. "The orphanage had to have a name on the books so they just called me Concho. Smith was just a name they gave me, too—you know, just a real common name."

I didn't look at her, but I knew she had sat up in the grass and was looking at me. "Did you ever find out anything about your parents or how you happened to be out there alone?"

"No," I said. "Nothing. My folks probably died, or more likely they were killed by Indians, but no one ever knew—at least if they did, they never told me about it."

"That's terrible," she said. "I mean, not knowing who you really are."

I shrugged and turned my head to look at her. "Well . . . I'm really Concho Smith, and I don't think much about where the name came from anymore."

"Have you been a loner and a drifter all your life?"

I smiled at her. "Who said anything about being a loner?"

"No one," she said. "But I can tell."

I sat up. "Well, I don't know—maybe you're right. Other than growing older and having a pretty frequent change of scenery, my life hasn't changed much in the past"—I thought about it a second—"in the past thirty-five years. Thirty-five years! My gosh, where'd it all go?"

"Yeah," Judith said softly. "Where does it go?"

I stood up. "I guess I'd better get old Drifter's shoes reset."

"Is that what you call the sorrel?" she asked, looking up at me.

"Yeah," I said, stepping over to Drifter and putting a hand on his rump, "this is ol' Drifter." I looked around and said, "This is a nice place—a nice ranch—at least judging from what I've seen of it from the outside fence . . . How long have you and Sid been married?"

Judith stood up and picked up the tray along with the empty glasses and lemonade pitcher.

Then she looked at me and said, "What you're really wanting to know is if I was a mail-order bride like Sid said on the way home, isn't it?"

"It's none of my business."

"I came here a little over a year ago," she said matter-of-factly, "and yes, Sid and I met through a company in Omaha. Some people *would* say that the company dealt in mail-order brides, but I never really thought of myself as actually being one. What other people choose to think is their business. Sid had his accident about five weeks after I came just two weeks after the wedding."

"That's a rough go," I said.

Judith nodded her head slowly, looking off into the distance. "Yes . . . ," she said. "I'd better go see about Sid—see if the liquor's wore off yet."

"Thanks for the lemonade," I said.

"Oh, you're welcome, Concho," she said. "It was good to get out of the house and just sit and talk."

CHAPTER 4

THE NEXT MORNING was still and cool, and even at midday it wasn't as hot as it had been for the past couple of weeks. Most cowboys like prowling in a new country and seeing new creeks and springs and canyons and such and that's what I was doing, but of course, I was looking for horses or horse sign all the time, too.

41

I was working my way around the foot of Big Butte Mesa, looking for a trail going up to the top. The sides of the mesa were steep and rocky, and the rimrock that capped it was about ten or twelve feet straight up and down and at least four hundred feet from the basin floor. The mesa was about two miles long and a mile wide, angling a little northeast and southwest. I knew there should be at least a thousand acres or so on top, and if there was water up there, too, and I was a horse, that's where I'd probably be.

I started on the east end and worked my way around the north side. The country along the foot of the mesa was rocky as the dickens and cut with deep washes that made the going slow. I found two little springs back in the shade, but one of them had completely dried up and the other wasn't running enough water in half an hour to fill a coffee cup. There were horse tracks at both of them, but they were old.

The country off the west end of the mesa was even rougher than that along the north side. It was steeper, and there were more prickly pear and cholla that a man had to pick his way through. It was mostly red dirt and rocks and cactus and bear grass and deep washes and sparse grass. But I was able to pick up a trail there that rimmed along the sloping foot and helped me and the little dun work our way around the west end. I had to get off only twice to lead him through the most treacherous places. The trail had fresh cattle and deer tracks on it, but no horse tracks at all.

The trail began rising and winding its way through boulders, some of which were taller than a man on a horse, working its way toward a sharp angle that would be the southwest corner of the mesa. I stopped to let the dun blow just before we reached the angle, and by then we were a quarter of the way up the side of the mesa itself. I figured that when we got around the corner I would see the trail angling up all the way to the top.

But instead of winding its way up a steep slope through rocks and cactus, the trail led down onto a pretty little bench, lower than where I was but higher than the basin floor. The bench was about a hundred yards wide and maybe three hundred yards long, covered with tall cedars and huge cottonwoods. There were a few head of cattle on the bench.

The back of the bench was a hundred-foot sheer rock cliff and in front of it, nestled among the trees, was a small cabin. Although I couldn't see any water from where I was, I knew there had to be a spring there somewhere.

There were three different trails leading up to the bench from the basin floor, and I could also see a trail coming out of the north side and working its way all the way to the top of the mesa. If I were a horse not wanting to go back to the horse pasture, and if there wasn't any water up on top of the mesa, then I'd come down that trail in the afternoon and drink and lounge in the shade of the cedars and cottonwoods.

I rode on down to the bench and found not just a good spring, but as near perfect a spring as I'd ever seen, and there were plenty of fresh horse tracks around it, too.

I rode the dun into the shade of the rock wall and up to the pool of clear water, which was about twelve feet across at the base. The dun snorted a time or two, then reached down to smell the water. I tossed him some slack in the reins and let him get a drink and then hobbled him while I drank from the spring myself.

The pool was fed by springwater coming from the bluff in several places starting about six feet off the ground up to a height of about ten feet. In places, it just seeped out of the rock, in other places it dripped, and in a few places it ran out in streams the size of a small twig. Most of the face of the wall was covered with dark green ferns that were dripping with water.

The sun would shine on the pool when it was straight overhead, but in the mornings it would be shaded by the trees and in the afternoons it would be shaded by the mesa. From the pool, the water ran down a cow trail to the edge of the bench, then spread out on the slope and disappeared just after reaching the basin floor into a wire trap that had about a half-section in it. The gates in the trap were open so cattle could go back and forth to water.

The cabin was an old one-room affair built beside the pool. It was about twenty feet long and twelve feet wide and made of cedar logs that were slick and shiny on the corners where cattle had been rubbing on them, as were the posts holding up the porch. Behind the cabin was a small corral, three sides of which were cedar pickets laced together with cowhide, the back side being the rock bluff. The west end of the cabin was all but covered by grapevines from the ground to the rusting tin on the roof. Inside the cabin was a rock fireplace, an old square table with three cowhide-bottomed chairs, two open-faced cabinets on the walls holding scarce canned goods and cookware, and an old iron bed with a felt mattress on top of flat wire springs and three blankets folded on the mattress. Two windows on each side of the door let in plenty of light and also gave a good view of both the basin to the south and the south rim rising some ten miles away.

I stepped back outside, sat on the edge of the porch, and rolled a smoke, enjoying being there. There was a nice coolness to the air coming from the spring along with the smell of damp leaves. Birds were singing in the trees, and one of the cows I'd boogered off the bench was bawling for her calf. The whole affair—bench, cabin, and spring—was as peaceful a place as I'd seen in a long time. But I didn't have time to admire it any longer. I stood up, unhobbled the dun, and started him up the trail that led from the north end of the bench to the top of the mesa.

By the time I got back to the house the sun was almost down. Judith came out of the house and to the corrals as I was closing the gate.

"Hi," she said with a warm smile. "Where'd you find them?"

"Up on top of Big Butte Mesa. I knew from the tracks they were up there, but it took me a while to find 'em."

She nodded. "I was beginning to wonder if the thought of those pretty señoritas waiting for you got to be more than you could stand and you'd gone on to Mexico after all. Sid wants you to eat supper with us."

I looked at her.

"He's actually drunk very little today and is in a decent mood," she said. "It'll be on the table by the time you wash up."

I washed up and shaved, changed my shirt, and combed my hair and mustache. "Come on in, Concho," I heard Judith say as I stepped up to the porch and raised my hand to knock on the screen door.

I hung my hat on the deer-antler rack just inside the door and stepped into the front room. It was filled with fine furnishings—a large sofa and nice parlor tables on each end and fancy banquet lamps on each table. Two stuffed chairs matched the sofa, and the floor was waxed hardwood. Across the room was a rock fireplace with tall glass-fronted bookcases on both sides. Behind the sofa was a china cabinet filled with pretty dishes and on the north wall was a fancy sideboard.

"Nice house," I said as I stepped into the kitchen where Sid was sitting at the table.

"Yeah . . . ," Sid replied. "I did it all for Judith. Sit down."

We ate in silence at a drop-leaf oak table set underneath a chandelier with three crystal globes. Judith was wearing a white blouse and a dark skirt, and her hair was pulled back and held in place with a turquoise-mounted comb. She looked so pretty that I couldn't keep my eyes from drifting across the table to her. Once, when I glanced up to look at her, she was looking at me and we both looked away quickly. The house was still warm when we began eating, but by the time we were finishing, an evening breeze had begun to move the west-wall curtains and dry the small drops of sweat on my forehead and upper lip.

"Get me and Concho a cigar," Sid said when Judith was pouring the coffee.

"How old are you?" Sid asked after the cigars had been lit and Judith had sat back down at the table.

"Forty-seven," I said.

"And where all have you been?"

" 'Bout ever'where," I answered.

"Ever go up the trail?" he asked.

"Yeah," I said. "To the railheads in Kansas several times and to Montana three times."

Sid barely nodded his head as he took the cigar out of his mouth and looked at it. "Who for?"

"Hutchinson, Saunders, Lytle and McDaniel, Lewis, King, and a few others," I said.

"So far as I know," Sid said, putting the cigar back into his mouth, "there hasn't been a real trail drive since ninety-five—what've you been doing since then?"

"Just cowboyin'," I said.

"Where?"

I laughed a little. "Ever'where."

He nodded again. "And what do you have to show for forty-seven years of living and all those trips up the trail and that cowboyin' everywhere?"

I looked at him. "Two saddle horses and a saddle and bedroll."

"You ever been drunk in a cow-town saloon?"

I glanced at Judith. "Yeah," I said.

"Ever paid for any in a cow-town whorehouse?"

Judith stood up and left the room.

I didn't answer.

"Have you found those other two horses yet?" Sid asked.

"Yeah," I said. "Today. On top of Big Butte."

Sid nodded again and was silent for a few

seconds, then he said, "It must be a real comedown to a big-outfit cowboy like yourself to be working on a little place like this—and all that fencing too. Mex'can work, wouldn't you say?"

I looked at him and thought about telling him to go to hell, but instead grinned and said, "It's a job."

"Well," he said and sort of laughed, "I guess we're fixing to find out what kind of hand you really are, Concho Smith—see if you've really been up the trail all those times and cowboyed everywhere. Little Bob—Shiner—sent a hand over here today and said they were going to throw a big roundup together two days from today at the mouth of Smokey Hill Creek, just this side of Smokey Hill, and they figure on having some of my cows in it. I want you to go over there as my rep . . . Leave tomorrow and be there the next morning to help them with the last day's gathering. Do you know where Smokey Hill is?"

"No," I said, "and I don't give a damn, either."

"I need a rep at Shiner's for a couple of days. But I don't want you going over there and embarrassing me."

"You can go to hell," I said, standing up.

"As you can see I can't rep for myself."

"That's not my problem. I don't care if you have a damn rep over there or not."

"But I need to get my cows home."

49

"Then you'd better hire some gunsel who'll put up with your bullshit."

"Proud bastard, aren't you?"

I shrugged. "Yeah."

"And a poor one, too," he said.

"Absolutely," I said as I started for the door.

"Where are you going?"

"To roll my bed and saddle my horses," I said.

"Okay . . . ," he said. "I'll give you five dollars a day to go over there."

I stopped at the hat rack only long enough to put my hat on before opening the screen door.

"Wait!" he said. "You mean you won't go over there for five dollars a day?"

"You couldn't pay me enough to go over there, Sid," I said.

"Look, goddammit, *I need* you to go to Shiner's and rep for me because I can't, and I don't have time to hire somebody else! I'm not going to beg you, though—I'll let every damn cow I own die at Shiner's before I'd do that!"

I stood there holding the screen door open and looking at him for a long time. "Draw me a map showing me where Smokey Hill is," I said, "and I'll go over there—for nothin'."

"For nothing? Hell, I'll—"

"Take it or leave it," I said. "I said you couldn't pay me enough to go over there, and I meant it."

He looked at me awhile and then glanced down the hallway and yelled, "Judith—get me some

50

paper and a pencil so I can draw Concho a map!"
Then he said, "I'd appreciate it if you'd ride my
horses while you're there. That bay with the star
and white left sock will really watch a cow."

I nodded and walked outside, rolled a cigarette,
and leaned against one of the posts on the porch
to smoke it. In a few minutes I heard the screen
door open and turned to see Judith holding Sid's
map.

As I took the note from her, our eyes met for a
moment, and then she went inside.

The next morning I shod three more Van horses,
and a little past noon left for Shiner's, riding one
Van horse and leading two others, one carrying
my bedroll. Sid was sitting on the porch watching
me when I left, but I never looked in his direction.

Not long after going through a gate in the
outside fence, I came upon Smokey Hill Creek
and the fork in it that Sid had drawn on the map.
Following the right-hand fork, I soon came to the
wagon road that was beside it and rode west for
about five miles until I saw the Shiner wagon
about a half mile east of Smokey Hill, the top of
which looked like the highest point in the basin
except for Big Butte Mesa.

The fly had been put on the wagon, and bedrolls
and teepees were scattered around it. It was late in
the day by then, and the day's work was finished.
A few cowboys were lounging about in the shade
of the fly telling wild-cow tales while the others

were day herding some cattle a little ways east of the wagon. The men at the wagon watched me ride up and one of them stepped out to meet me.

"I'm Concho Smith—reppin' for Sid Van," I said.

"Mr. Shiner said Sid ought to have a man comin'," the cowboy said as he eased up to the left side of my horse and stuck out his hand. "I'm Shiner's wagon boss—Otto Brooks. You're welcome to throw your horses in with the remuda if you want."

"Thanks," I said, "but I think I'll just hobble 'em."

"Suit yourself," Brooks said. "You don't want 'em skinned up by a bunch of ill-natured, long-toothed remuda horses, huh?"

I grinned. "I'd just as soon they weren't."

"Make yourself at home. We've got one more day's gatherin'," he said, "and then we'll work the herd day after tomorrow. Glad to have you with us . . . there's no drinkin' or gamblin' at the wagon. Supper will be ready pretty quick."

I rode out a ways from the wagon, where I hobbled the horses and unloaded my bedroll. By then the cook was already yelling, "Supper!"

Most of the cowboys were already eating when I stepped underneath the fly. I didn't look at them individually, just gave them a nod and a quick howdy and began filling my plate.

"Get that fence all fixed up?" someone said. I

looked around and saw that it was Billy Wright. He was sitting on the ground next to Malcolm Floyd and wearing a cocky smile that showed off a nice set of teeth underneath a long nose.

"Hello, Billy . . . Malcolm," I said. "Yeah . . . I got 'er in pretty good shape."

"How about that mail-order bride?" Floyd said.

I looked at him. I didn't like him the first time I met him and I was liking him even less now. "Her name's Judith Van," I said. "If you're askin' how she is, as far as I know she's fine."

"Yeah," Floyd said with a crooked smile. "She sure is that all right."

"Find the rest of them horses?" Billy asked.

"Got 'em all back home," I said as I finished filling my plate.

"You come over here to get Sid's cattle?"

"Yeah," I said as I poured coffee into a tin cup and stepped out from underneath the fly and carried my plate to my bedroll.

As I was eating, I looked up to see a short, stocky cowboy carrying his plate toward me. I couldn't believe it. It was Shorty Wayman.

"Hello, you worthless, driftin' piece of human flotsam!" he said.

I stood up, then reached out and shook his hand. "Well, I'll be damned—what 'n the hell are you doing here, Shorty? I haven't seen you in three or four years."

"Since we were in the Simon country in

Arizona," Shorty said. "What're you doin' way down here?"

"I asked you first," I said.

"Well . . ." Shorty was a lot longer in words than he was in height. "I've been askin' myself that very same damn thing for about a month now—that's how long I've been here—and the only answer I've come up with is that I guess since I'd never been here before I thought I ought to come."

"It don't look like a bad sort of country," I said.

"Hell no," he said, "the country's just fine, and Shiner pays thirty-five a month, but it's all these damn home guards that I can't stomach . . . but I guess things are changin' ever'where. I think you're the first son of a bitch I've seen since I've been here that's ever punched cows anywhere but right here in this one little basin, and they think that if you haven't cowboyed here then you haven't cowboyed at all . . . Well, I've told the wretched tale about why I'm here. What about you?"

"I was on my way to Mexico," I said, "and one of Shiner's neighbors—Sid Van—put me up in his barn for the night a couple of weeks ago and I'm still there. I'm over here reppin' for him."

"I've heard about Sid Van and his good-lookin' mail-order bride," Shorty said. "I guess he was a mighty good hand before he got crippled up."

I shrugged. "He's got some pretty good horses—at least for fencin'."

"So," Shorty asked, "have you given up on Mexico?"

"Hell no! I'll be pulling out just as soon as I'm done here," I said.

Shorty stood up with his empty plate in his hand. "I've got my teepee set up over there on the other side of the wagon in the low-rent district—why don't you bring your bedroll over there and we'll build a fire and tell wild-cow tales."

We talked till way past dark about cowboys and horses and outfits we knew. After the fire had died out and we were lying in our bedrolls, Shorty said, "You want company on that little jaunt across the border you're goin' on?"

"Sure," I said. "You're more 'n welcome to come."

"I've been to Mexico once," he said, "but I think, by damn, I left one gal in one little cantina completely undiddled."

I laughed. "I'm disappointed in you, Shorty—it's not like you to leave a job undone like that."

"Just let me know when you're pullin' out," he said, "and we'll bid these home-guardin', mare-ridin', staple-drivin', square-bread-eatin' sons-abitches a fond adios."

"Sounds good to me," I said.

CHAPTER 5

THE NEXT DAY we made a pretty good circle and gathered quite a few cattle. I saw a few Van cows in the bunch, too, and they all had calves sucking them, but none of the calves were branded. While me and Shorty were sitting in front of his teepee waiting for supper, a buckboard pulled up to the wagon. "That's the new big he-dog of the outfit—Robert Shiner," Shorty said.

"Or," I said, "as Sid calls him—Little Bob."

"One and the same," Shorty said. "Only I guess Sid's the only one with enough balls to call him that to his face . . . Damn, I hope old Malcolm don't break a leg gettin' to him," he added as we saw Malcolm Floyd rush out from underneath the fly to greet the buckboard before it had even come to a stop.

"Malcolm may be your next wagon boss," I chided.

"Yeah," Shorty chuckled, "and if that wagon had wings it could fly, too. Otto may not be the best hand in the world but he's a damn sight better than anybody else drawin' Shiner wages, and he's not all that bad of a feller either."

We watched Floyd shake hands with Robert Shiner while Otto Brooks walked out to the buckboard, then the three of them walked back underneath the fly.

"Let's ease on over to the fly, too," Shorty said as he stood up. "We don't want to be very far from the front of the chuck line when Cookie hollers."

Underneath the fly most of the Shiner cowboys were spinning yarns again and talking about the day's gathering while they waited for supper. "Concho," Billy Wright said—he was standing next to Robert Shiner just underneath the edge of the fly—"we were trying to figure out how many cattle we lost today. Were those two pair that got away from you along the creek the only ones you spilled?"

It's not out of the ordinary for cowboys to heckle each other about the day's events, the way they handle cattle or horses or nearly anything else—but it's usually done good-naturedly and with a certain respect. This was a different kind of country, though, with a different kind of hand in it, as me and Shorty had said. And just like nearly every time he'd had anything at all to say to me, I couldn't have picked out any respect in Billy Wright's voice even if I tried, which I wasn't in the mood to do. "I didn't spill a goddamn thing," I said, looking him right in the eye. "I was flankin' Shorty up—those cows come out behind me, not in front of me."

"Hell," Billy said, "all you had to've done was to rein that wonderful son of a bitch of a Van horse around and head 'em!" which brought a round of chuckles from the rest of the hands.

I smiled and shook my head. It was hard to believe that any man drawing cowboy wages would say such a stupid thing. "Billy," I said, "I didn't spill the sonsabitches. If you'd been flankin' me up like you should have . . ."

Billy glanced at Robert Shiner and stiffened before he looked back at me and said, "You're saying it was my fault?"

"Absolutely," I said in as flat a voice as I could, looking him right in the eye.

"Well . . . I'll be goddamn," he said, taking a step toward me. "You go from Mexican fencer to head cowboy in a few days on a little nester place and all of a sudden you think you savvy how to punch cows on a real cow outfit?"

"Git it!" the cook hollered, trying to head off what looked like was coming.

I leaned over and picked a plate up and started filling it with Billy Wright's eyes burning holes in my back. But I didn't care—lately, I'd got to where I was feelin' about fighting like I was about riding pitching horses . . . I'd just as soon not.

"Hey, goddammit!" Billy said. "I'm still talkin' to you!"

I finished filling my plate and carried it over to Shorty's teepee and sat cross-legged on the ground to eat. In a minute Shorty came over and sat next to me on the ground and started eating, too. I was about half through with my plate when I looked over at him and he shook his head.

58

I went back to work on the food on my plate and a couple of minutes later, without looking up, said, "I'll be damned if I'll flank you up again."

Shorty chuckled for a few seconds, then started laughing so hard he fell onto his back, holding his sides.

We both laughed awhile and then Shorty sat up and wiped the tears from his eyes, took a couple of deep breaths, and said, "I figured you were about to dot Billy Wright's cowpunchin' eye."

"I thought about it," I said, "but I wasn't much in the mood to get all skinned up . . . besides, the last thing Sid Van said to me was that he hoped I didn't embarrass him over here."

Shorty looked over at me, and I could tell he was having all he could do to keep from busting out laughing again. "He didn't either," he said.

I nodded my head.

"Naw . . ."

"On a stack of Bibles, Shorty," I told him.

Shorty fell onto his back again, laughing and trying to say something, but his words came out like he had his mouth full of marbles.

I turned my head and saw two pairs of boots in front of me. Everything under the sun was funny right then. Every word and every look and everything me or Shorty saw was just another reason to laugh, or to keep laughing—even two pairs of boots.

Through my tear-blurred eyes I was finally able

to make out Billy Wright's and Robert Shiner's forms filling those boots. I tried to say something but couldn't. Billy Wright said something but I had no idea what it was. I shut my eyes, took a deep breath, and tried again. I let the air out of my lungs slowly, bit my lip, and made sure to look at Billy instead of Shorty. I hadn't planned on saying what I did—I just opened my mouth and out it came: "Hello, you cowpunchin' fool, you," I said, which turned out to be so damn funny me and Shorty were plumb beside ourselves again.

Billy Wright said something else, but again I was laughing so hard I had no idea what it was. What he said next though, I did hear: "Hey, goddammit . . . when I talk to you, you'd better stand up and pay attention to me, you son of a bitch!"

All of a sudden I cared a lot less about getting skinned up than I did just a few minutes ago.

I stopped laughing as best I could and stood up.

I don't know what Billy was thinking I was going to do, but it must have been that I was going to stand up and pay attention to him just like he'd said I'd better, because when I hit him he was standing there limber as a rag doll without a single muscle in his body tightened up.

The immediate effect of that punch surprised me almost as much as it did him because, for a cowboy, I'd always been even farther down on the fighting scale than I was on the bronc-riding scale. I'd been known to hit men before who just blinked their eyes and looked at me. But not Billy—when my fist hit the corner of his mouth his head snapped back, his knees buckled, and he dropped like he'd been kicked in the head by a mule.

"Damn!" Shorty said, still sitting on the ground and looking up at me. "Where'd you get that?"

I looked at my fist and shrugged.

Billy lay as still as a stripped cedar post.

I looked at Robert Shiner and stuck my hand out to him. "Mr. Shiner, I'm Concho Smith. I'm reppin' for Sid Van."

Shiner looked at my hand and then he looked down at Billy, who was beginning to wiggle a little bit. When he looked back at me, he seemed to be at a loss for anything to say.

Malcolm Floyd, Otto Brooks, and several other hands came rushing over to us. By then Shorty was on his feet and Billy was on his knees. "What the hell's going on here?" Otto asked.

"Billy was askin' for it, Otto," Shorty said.

"You work for me don't you, Wayman?" Shiner asked.

"Yeah . . . sure," Shorty answered.

"Do you know this man?"

"Concho? . . . Sure."

"I mean did you know him before he went to work for Sid Van?"

"Hell . . . I've known Concho for fifteen years at least."

By then a couple of Shiner men had helped

Billy to his feet. He jerked away from them and charged me like a bull, butting his head into my stomach and shoving me backward faster than I could run in that direction. I could tell I was fixing to fall and figured it would be better if I went ahead and did it on my own accord than waiting a second and letting Billy do it to me.

I grabbed Billy's shirt collar at the back of his neck with my right hand and fell over, but I twisted my body to the left and pushed Billy toward the ground as I did so. I landed hard on my right side, but Billy landed even harder and on his face. I rolled and came up on my feet.

"Otto!" Shiner yelled.

"That's enough!" Otto shouted, and then, "Boys, get ahold of 'em!"

It must have been an oversight on somebody's part because it seemed like the whole Shiner crew grabbed me but somehow neglected to do the same for Billy—who came up cussing and swinging and landed a fist in my left eye.

Otto said, "Goddammit, Billy! Stop!" but it took Shorty flying into him from behind and knocking him into us to keep me from welcoming Billy's flailing fists again.

I jerked my arms loose and was there waiting for Billy when he got to his feet again, but before I could hit him, Otto came between us. "That's it!" he said, looking at me. "There ain't gonna be any fightin' at the wagon." Then he turned toward

Billy and said, "That goes for you too, Billy—now you get on over there to your teepee. Everybody, just go on—it's over!"

Billy glared at me a moment and then walked away with the rest of the Shiner cowboys, telling them how I had hit him by surprise.

"I guess I shouldn't be surprised that Sid would send somebody like you over here," Robert Shiner said.

I looked at him but didn't say anything.

"I want Sid's cattle off my place all right, but if you cause any more trouble, I'll send you home and we'll cut Sid's cattle out without a rep here and take 'em back ourselves. I was just trying to be neighborly, but I'm not going to put up with some . . . some malcontent Sid sends over here. Is that clear?"

I didn't know what to do but to stretch my mustache into a smile. "A mal . . . what?" I asked.

Shiner looked at me for a few seconds and then him and Otto and Malcolm Floyd walked toward the wagon fly. When they got to the fly they talked for a little while more, and then Shiner and Floyd got back in the buckboard and left.

I looked at Shorty and neither of us could do anything but shake our heads and smile. "Thanks for the help," I said.

"Aw hell," he said, "it wasn't my intention to help, I was just trying to get out of the way and fell into Billy."

The working of the herd began the next morning just after sunup at the foot of Smokey Hill. I was riding the bay Sid had said would watch a cow. Otto trotted around the herd to where I was and rode up beside me. "Ordinarily, I'd let you in the herd first, Concho," he said, "but Mr. Shiner gave strict orders to not cut out any Van stock until he got here. We've already got his horse saddled for 'im and I guess he'll be here before long. For now, though, I guess I'd better do like he said. I'll get Malcolm to help me, and we'll go ahead and start cutting out our big steers."

After about a hundred head of Shiner steers big enough for slaughter had been cut out, I saw a wagon coming in from the east, but when it got close enough I could see that it was not Robert Shiner—it was Sid and Judith.

When the wagon pulled around to my side of the herd, I trotted out to it. Sid was in his cowboy clothes, and he did have a cowboy look about him, despite being crippled and sitting on a wagon seat.

"At least they don't have you holding up the cuts," he said in a good-natured tone. "Every now and then old Bob would do that to me for spite." Then he got a good look at my face and saw the black eye Billy Wright had given me. "What 'n the hell happened to you?"

I smiled. "I ran into a tent pole . . . Otto said we

64

couldn't cut out any of your stock until Shiner got here." I relaxed in the saddle and let the bay I was riding stand on a loose rein while I looked at Judith and said, "Good mornin'." She was wearing a gray riding skirt and a muslin blouse, and her hair was pulled back and tied with a ribbon.

Then I noticed the saddle in the back of the wagon. "Judith can ride one of the horses you brought over and help you drive the cattle home," Sid said.

"That is," Judith said, with her lips turned up in a mocking smile, "if you're not . . . too proud."

"Little Bob should have been here at daylight," Sid grumbled. "His old daddy sure would've been."

Something toward the east caught my eye, and I twisted in the saddle for a better look. "Yonder comes another wagon now," I said.

We watched as the wagon pulled around the herd to where we were and stopped ten feet away. It was Robert Shiner.

"Well, if it's not the Vans," Shiner said. "Come over to protect your interest, Sid?"

"I'm as anxious to get my cattle home as you are to get rid of them, Little Bob," Sid said.

"I doubt it," Shiner came back in an irritated tone. "After all, you're the one who's been getting the free grass, not me."

"There's some of your cattle on my land, too—

but now that the fence is fixed, Concho can start throwing 'em out."

"Maybe I ought to send my crew over and gather your place for you, Sid. They could probably do it in one day, no bigger than it is—we could even brand your calves for you."

"If I need your help, Little Bob, I'll let you know—until then I'd just as soon your boys stayed off my place."

"Kinda funny, isn't it, that I let you come over here to protect your interest, but you don't want me sending my men over there?"

"Little Bob, if my place was as big as yours, I'd be glad for you to send some men over. Like I said—if I need your help, I'll let you know."

"Well . . . ," Shiner mulled, nodding his head slowly, "we'll see. Things are going to be different from here on, Sid. One reason I'm gathering everything now is so I can take an inventory. Daddy was set in his ways and was still running things like he did in the old days, still keeping books in his mind or on the back of a glove. He never knew for sure exactly how many cattle he had, and you know as well as I do that some people have taken advantage of that fact."

"Meaning me?" The good-natured tone Sid had in his voice when he'd gotten there was now gone.

"Meaning whoever it applies to, Sid."

Malcolm Floyd came out of the herd, where

he'd been cutting out slaughter steers, and stopped between Robert Shiner's and Sid's wagons. "Good morning, Mr. Shiner," he said. "I'll go saddle your horse for you."

"Never mind, Malcolm," Shiner said. "Otto's saddling him."

Floyd twisted in his saddle and turned toward Sid's wagon, looking down at Judith. "How are you, Mrs. Van?" he asked.

"I'm fine," Judith said without looking at him.

Otto came trotting up to the wagon, leading Shiner's horse, a big, good-looking gray. Shiner got out of the wagon and got on the horse, then trotted around the wagon and stopped beside me.

"Little Bob, this is Concho Smith," Sid said.

"I know who the hell he is," Shiner growled. "I started to send him home last night . . . I'll let him in the herd with me and Otto and Malcolm to start with, and we'll see how he does. If he stirs the cattle up too much, he'll have to get out and we'll cut your stock for you."

"The arrogant bastard!" Sid said when Shiner, Brooks, and Floyd trotted off. "What'd he mean by that?"

"He means he don't put up with malcontents like me," I said.

Sid looked at me and smiled. "I'm sorta beginning to like you," he said.

"Better be careful, I don't think that's allowed around here," I said as I reined the bay around and eased him into the milling herd. Before long, I spotted a Hereford cow with Sid's under-slope earmark in her left ear.

I eased around to the cow's left side and saw that she had Sid's "V" on her hip and started working her out. She was an old high-horned, freckled faced thing with a wild look about her, so when I got her—along with three Shiner cows —to the edge of the herd, I stopped to give her some air and let her settle down.

The bay stood quiet on a slack rein, but his ears were flicking back and forth toward the cows and I knew this was not the first herd of cattle he'd been in by a long shot.

Malcolm Floyd came trotting up behind me. "Better not cut her out without her calf," he said.

I twisted in the saddle and looked back to see if he was serious, and for all the world it looked like he was. "She doesn't have a calf," I said.

"You'd better look at her again."

"She had a calf and lost it," I told him. "She's dryin' up—she hasn't been sucked in a week."

Just then Robert Shiner came trotting up. "What's wrong?" he asked.

"He was going to cut that wet cow out without her calf," Malcolm said.

"Well, damn, Smith," Shiner said, "you gotta pair 'em up before you can cut 'em out. Jesus Christ!"

"I'll bet you a hundred dollars she don't have a calf," I said.

"How much of this bullshit are you going to put up with, Mister Shiner?" Malcolm asked.

"None!" he said. Then he looked straight at me. "*Don't* cut that cow out without her calf!"

Otto saw us palavering and rode over to us. "Something wrong?"

"He was goin' to cut that Van cow out without her calf," Shiner said.

Otto trotted thirty feet to the side so he could get a better look at the cow and then trotted back. "She's lost her calf," he said.

"Well . . . ," Shiner said looking at Floyd, "I couldn't see her very good. I was just going by what Malcolm said."

"I still don't think I'm wrong," Floyd said. "I'll bet the bitch comes back to the herd bawling for her calf."

"Go ahead and cut her out, Concho," Otto said.

I smiled and nodded and eased the bay toward the cows.

The Van cow threw her head up and started trotting toward the right with three Shiner cows following her. The bay shuffled his feet, and the instant I lifted the reins he jumped in front of the cows and they stopped.

The old high-horned Van cow couldn't stand to be still and moved to the right again, but this time the Shiner cows didn't go with her. I backed the bay up to give her some air and time to get a little farther away from the Shiner cows. When there were about twenty feet between her and the Shiner cows, I could tell she was about to break into a run, so I moved the bay forward a few steps.

But this time she didn't stop. She threw her head up and broke into a run. The bay dropped his front end and pivoted on his right hock and cut her off. She wheeled to the left without stopping, but the bay cut her off again. All I had to do was to sit up there on the bay and bump the curb against him every now and then so he wouldn't crowd her too much. She sashayed to the left again and back to the right, but the bay was quick as a cat and she'd have better luck trying to shed her tail than trying to get by him and back into the herd. The old cow was smart enough to figure this out herself, and although she didn't like it a bit, pretty soon she gave up trying to get back into the herd and moved toward the small herd of cuts a hundred yards away.

That bay was eat up with cow, no doubt about it, and I would have been proud to have been on him in any herd—but I was double proud to be on him in *that* herd because I knew Malcolm Floyd, Billy Wright, Robert Shiner, and everyone else were watching us.

I glanced toward Sid and Judith and both of them were smiling.

Otto, Robert Shiner, Malcolm Floyd, and myself each cut out a few more head of Van cattle before

I spotted a cow with a broken horn and a three-hundred-pound, ring-eyed, red-necked heifer following her. The calf was unbranded, but there was no doubt they were a pair. The cow acted pretty sensible, but that calf was nervous and flighty.

Three times I was able to keep the pair together and work them to the edge of the herd, but each time the calf would break away from the cow and return to the herd in a run. Twice the bay was right in front of the calf, but it didn't matter, there was no turn-back in her ring-eyed disposition. The third time the calf made her break back to the herd she ran right underneath my right stirrup.

As I was working the pair toward the edge of the herd for the fourth time, I took down my rope, dropped a loop over the saddle horn, pulled it tight, and shook out a loop in the other end.

I got them to the edge of the herd again and gave them plenty of air, trying to let the calf settle down so she would follow the cow out.

I heard someone yell, "Put that goddamn rope up, Smith—you'll scatter the whole herd!"

The calf broke away from the cow again and was going toward the herd in a hard run with her tail up over her back when I roped her with a hoolihand loop and drug out the slack with a satisfying "zip!"

The heifer bellowed and was running as hard as she could when she hit the end of the rope and came over backward.

That was when Robert Shiner arrived on the gray.

"Look out!" I yelled.

But the inevitable had already been set in motion. Shiner was caught between the calf on one end of the rope and me—tied hard and fast to the saddle horn—on the other end.

The calf jumped to her feet and swung toward the right on the end of the tight rope, bringing the rope against the gray's hocks. The gray gathered himself, snorted and kicked, broke wind, and came apart.

Shiner lasted two jumps before he landed on his back in the powdery dirt. The gray pitched through the herd with the stirrups of Shiner's saddle flopping over the saddle seat and scattering cattle.

When I saw that only Shiner's pride was injured, I led the calf toward the cuts with the cow following close behind and bawling to her.

Shorty come over and heeled the calf for me. "Well, you didn't stir the herd up much, Concho," he said with a laugh as he took the ropes off the calf, "but I'll bet Shiner's a little stirred up. Serves him right for not stayin' out of the goddamn way. Maybe now he'll stay out of the herd and let Otto run things."

Malcolm was handing the gray's reins to Shiner when I rode up to them. "I'm sorry, Mr. Shiner," I said, "but there wasn't a hell of a lot I could do about it."

"You shouldn't have had your damn rope down in the first place. Mr. Shiner told you to put the son of a bitch up!" Malcolm said.

"Well, Malcolm," I said, "askin' permission to take my rope down or put it up is a habit I guess I just never got around to developing."

Malcolm glared at me while Shiner dusted himself off and got back in the saddle. Then Shiner reined his gray toward Sid's wagon and stopped a few feet from it. He tried to speak calmly, but with very little success. "Sid . . . that was the last of your cows. I want them off Shiner land right now, and I don't ever intend on pasturing any more of 'em!"

"Oh hell, calm down, Little Bob," Sid said, not trying in any way to contain or conceal his delight. "Just because you got the round-ass and rolled off, don't go to talking crazy."

"Just get your cattle and get on out of here, Sid," Shiner said as he was riding away. "And I don't want Smith on Shiner land again, not ever!"

"Sorry about that, Sid," I said after Shiner had ridden off. "I didn't intend for that to happen."

"Well, I enjoyed the hell out of it myself. Why don't you put Judith's saddle on old Easy—that's what I call the little dun you brought over. We'll throw your bedroll in the wagon and tie the other two horses to the back and I'll lead 'em home."

CHAPTER 6

AFTER WE GOT back onto Van property we stopped our little bunch of cattle at a water hole. By then it was late in the day—the sun hadn't fallen below the horizon yet, but it was getting close to it.

"We left the gates open between here and the house," Sid said. "Hold 'em up until you think they're mammied-up good enough. I'm going on to the house."

The water hole was a spring off the west end of Big Butte Mesa. The hole was no more than twenty feet across with a big cottonwood tree at the edge. We held the cattle there for about half an hour after Sid left. Everything was calm—the calves were sucking and nothing was bawling any longer. A dove was cooing from somewhere down the creek.

I rode over beside Judith. "I think they're mammied-up okay," I said.

We started toward home, walking the horses. The sun had already dropped below the rim of the western world, but daylight was hanging on.

"Tired?" I asked.

"Yeah—my bottom's tired and my legs are sore. I haven't ridden this much in a long time. But it's been fun, Concho. Sid enjoyed it, too."

"Well . . . there *is* something special about

74

seein' a horse get out from under someone you don't like."

A coyote loped across in front of us and stopped on a hill a hundred yards away to watch us a few seconds before dropping his head and disappearing.

"I need to get away from the house more often," Judith said. "I get so tense since Sid got hurt that sometimes I forget how peaceful it is out here by yourself."

"I know I'm not much company," I said, "but . . ."

Judith laughed. "I didn't mean you weren't good company, Concho. It's just that with you there's nothing . . ."

"Yeah?"

She laughed again. "With you it's like being by myself without being alone."

"Yeah?" I said again.

"Oh, just shut up, Concho," she said. "I'm trying to pay you a compliment. Just say, 'Thank you, Judith'."

"Thank you, Judith," I said.

"You're welcome," she said and we both laughed.

We came to the division fence between the two pastures that made up the major portion of the ranch and I got off to shut the gate that Judith had opened when she and Sid came through that morning. By then, daylight was gone and no moon had risen to replace it in the star-filled sky.

"I've got to stretch my legs," Judith said and got off as I dropped the twisted wire keeper over the top of the gatepost. "Ouch! . . . Oh!"

"What's wrong?" I asked, turning around but unable to see much.

"Oh! I stepped right into a dang cactus! Ouch!"

"Let me see," I said, stepping toward her. We'd been on the wagon road, but she'd stepped off her horse just out of the wagon tracks and bumped into a cholla. I leaned over so I could see. "There's still a pod in your knee," I told her.

"Well, gee, Concho . . . I guess that's why it hurts so bad!" she said in a mocking tone.

"Just hold on a minute," I said as I reached into my pocket to get my pocket knife. "Don't try to pull it out or you'll get it in your hand."

I opened the long blade, put it underneath the cactus pod, and popped it out of her leg.

"Oh! Damn!"

"You're welcome," I said as I put the knife back into my pocket. "They got a little barb on the end of the thorns—that's why they hurt even more coming out than they do going in."

"Thanks," she said as she turned around and stepped back into the wagon tracks.

"You ready to go?"

"Yes, I guess so," she said.

"You don't sound sure."

"I think there's a thorn still in there," she said, pulling up the left leg of the riding skirt and leaning over to look. "Ouch! Yes, there is. I can't see it, but I sure can feel it. Let me see your knife."

"Let me get it out for you," I said.

She held the riding skirt up a few inches above her knee as I knelt in front of her. I put my hand just above her boot top and slid it up the smooth calf of her leg towards her knee.

"You're handling me like a horse, Concho—I'm not going to kick."

I smiled. "If you do, I'll have to tie a foot up."

"Ouch!"

"There it is . . . broke off and kind of short, but maybe I can get ahold of it with my knife. Hold real still."

She put her hand on my back to balance herself.

With my left hand behind her knee I flexed it a little and got my face close to it so I could see better, which wasn't very good in that dim light.

"What're you doing? Am I going to have to pull it out myself?"

"Just hold on . . . This isn't the best surgical light in the world, you know." I pressed the thorn against the knife blade with my thumb and jerked it out with the first try. It had been in a good quarter inch. "There. How does that feel?"

She rubbed her knee with her hand. "Better. I think that must have been the only one. Thanks . . . Dr. Smith."

I stood up and put the knife into my pocket

again. We were standing close to each other now, so close I could look down and see the reflection of the stars twinkling in her eyes. She took a deep breath and stepped back.

"You ready to go now?" I asked.

"Yes," she said. "We'd better get home—Sid may still be sitting in the wagon waiting for us."

The wagon was at the yard gate when we got back, but Sid wasn't in it. The house was dark, too.

"Sid!" Judith yelled. "Sid! . . . Sid!"

He didn't answer.

"God . . . ," Judith said, "I wonder where he is?" She got off her horse and ran around the wagon and through the yard gate. I tied the horses to the wagon bed and followed her, but heard her say as I walked through the gate, "Why didn't you answer me?"

Sid was sitting in his chair in the dark on the porch. I could barely see him, even though I was standing at the foot of the porch steps.

"What'n the hell you been doing?" he asked.

"We held the cattle up for a while and then we came home," Judith said.

"Then you should've been here an hour ago."

"Why didn't you answer me?"

"Do you know how hard it was for me to get out of the wagon and into the house by myself?"

"Looks like you made it to the liquor cabinet okay."

"Yeah, I did! And why not?"

I didn't figure they needed me so I went back out the gate, climbed up into the wagon seat, unwrapped the lines from around the brake handle, and started the team toward the barn.

The next morning there was no movement around the house even after the sun had come up. I finally caught a horse and trotted over to the water hole where we'd turned the cattle loose the afternoon before to see if everything was still mammied-up. Most of the cattle were either grazing on the flat beside the water hole or up the creek a little ways from it. One pair I didn't see though, was the ring-eyed, red-necked heifer I'd had to drag out of the herd and her mammie, so I decided to trot on over to the back fence—the one between Sid's land and the Smokey Hill country of Shiner's where the pair had been running.

As I got to the edge of a big plum thicket, I saw them before they saw me—the cow was grazing about thirty feet off the fence and the calf was lying in the grass close to her. They were still on Sid's side of the fence, all right—but for how long? They definitely had going back to Smokey Hill on their minds, and four-strand barbed-wire fences are good for keeping gentle stock at home, but not much beyond that. To make matters worse, that heifer wasn't branded. If the pair got back to Smokey Hill and were still there when the cow kicked the calf off, which she would sooner or later, then Sid would have no way to claim the calf.

Although for all I knew I was still working without wages, I decided to do what I'd have done if the cattle were mine—I'd rope the calf and build a fire and brand her with the branding ring I had tied to my saddle. That way, even if she did get back on Shiner's land, Sid could still claim her.

I got off and tightened my cinches, got back on, and took my rope down. I had to come out of the plum thicket, but I did so leaning over the saddle horn and riding at an easy trot. I didn't want them to see me until I had swung around and got on the fence myself. That way when they boogered, they would booger away from those four puny strands of barbed wire.

But as luck would have it, that old cow saw me before I'd covered thirty feet. The instant she threw her head up and stopped chewing, that little wild heifer jumped up and was running the minute all four feet were on the ground. And she didn't run but in one direction—straight toward the fence. She bounced off it once and cut her nose, hit it again—this time forefooting herself between the top two strands of wire—and wound up on the other side. She ran about fifty yards and then stopped and looked back with her head high and her ears thrown forward.

The cow had more sense than to run into the fence like her calf had, but she started trotting down it. The calf ran back to the fence and away they went in a long trot away from me on opposite sides of the fence from each other.

I muttered a few of the most vile words I could think of and headed for the gate, which was about a quarter mile in the opposite direction.

I opened the gate and threw it back, then went in a hard run in a half circle to my right on Shiner land, swinging way off the fence and then coming back to it when I was in front of the cow and calf. I stopped at the fence and let them come toward me until they saw me again and stopped. Then I talked as easy as my disposition at the moment would allow and they turned around and started trotting down the fence toward the gate.

I wanted the calf to get to the gate first and go back into Sid's country instead of the other way around, naturally, so when they were about fifty yards from the gate I started crowding the heifer. I didn't care a bit if I crowded her so much she ran back through the fence before she got to the gate.

But nothing hardly ever runs through a fence when you want it to, and that heifer sure wasn't any exception to that cow-country rule. And not only did she not crowd through the fence, when she got to the gate she threw her head up and took off, running away from it.

But that came as no big surprise, and as soon as

she did, I pointed the Van horse toward her butt, gave him a little steel in the ribs, and when he bumped her hocks I reared up and cut her throat with twisted hemp. I laid the slack down her back, and that horse planted his butt on Shiner sod and gave her a good dose of hemp therapy.

Nothing cures a sour cowboy disposition like thumping the back of something's head on the ground, especially something that's got her tail up over her back and headed for the tules. I wasn't even upset when the cow came trotting through the gate because I knew that when I led her bawling, slobbering, red-necked bundle of joy back through it, she would follow, which is exactly what happened.

When we were through the gate and back onto Sid's country, I let the calf step over the rope and bedded her down. My suddenly resurrected good humor didn't last long though, because when I was tying her down with my piggin' string I looked up just in time to see none other than my old friends Billy Wright and Malcolm Floyd trot up to the still-open gate and stop.

"For your sake," Billy said, "I hope that calf's wearin' a Van brand, because we seen you rope her on this side of the fence and drag her back through this gate."

"She's not wearin' a brand at all right now," I said as I stood up and took the rope off the calf's head. "But she's fixin' to be."

"And what brand is she fixin' to be wearin'?" Billy asked.

"Sid's V," I said. "She's Sid's calf."

"Says you?" Billy asked sarcastically.

"Says that cow right yonder peekin' through the plum bushes with the V on her hip and the swaller-fork in her left ear," I said. Nearly any cowboy would have recognized the calf as being one that was cut out of the herd at Smokey Hill the day before, especially since she was the one I had roped and the same one that rimfired Robert Shiner when he got in the way. But then I already knew what kind of hands Billy Wright and Malcolm Floyd were.

Malcolm was strangely quiet, but the way he was looking at me I could tell he wasn't over what had happened at Smokey Hill the day before.

Billy shook his head and grinned. "Caught red-handed ropin' an unbranded calf on Shiner land and about to put Sid's brand on her . . . This'll make Mr. Shiner real happy—especially after all the trouble you caused at the wagon."

"Well," I said, mustering all the sarcasm I could, "keepin' Mr. Shiner happy is something I sure aspire to do."

"Smart bastard, aren't you," Billy said.

"Naw . . . I've decided I don't have a lick of sense. If I did, I'd already be in a cantina in Mexico tryin' to impress some plump Mexican maiden with my gringo charm."

"Maybe you ought to just head for Mexico right now," Malcolm Floyd said in a dry tone.

"Yeah," I said. "But hell, since I already went to all the trouble to get this heifer back home and tied down I reckon I oughta just go ahead and brand her."

"Shorty said you'd cowboyed just about everywhere and were a hell of a hand," Billy said. "But I say bullshit on that, and I say bullshit on the way you snuck in that punch on me at the wagon." I looked down at the calf's feet and checked to make sure my huey was pulled tight. "Do you want to finish what we started?"

I sat down on the calf's belly, put my forearms on my knees, and looked up at him. "To tell you the truth, Billy," I said, "I'd just as soon not."

Billy grinned again. "That's what I thought."

I smiled back.

"Then drag that calf back through this gate and turn her loose."

"I thought we'd already been through that," I said.

"If you don't," Billy said, "I'm gonna really kick your worn-out old ass!"

I looked at him again and shook my head. "Well, I won't be able to say you didn't warn me."

"You sure as hell won't," he said as he trotted his horse through the gate.

"Damn," I said to no one in particular as I stood up.

As soon as Billy's feet hit the ground he bulled into me with his head down again and knocked me over the calf. He had two things going for him, youth and enthusiasm, whereas I had wisdom and experience. We'd been into it no time when I'd already decided that given the opportunity, a man would be a fool not to trade wisdom and experience for youth and enthusiasm.

I wasn't even aware that Floyd had trotted through the gate until the first time he hit me in the ribs with a club—cracked a couple of them and made my legs so wobbly I sunk to the ground on my knees, fighting for my breath.

That first blow from Floyd's club—it turned out to be a two-inch cedar stay—did more damage than the eight or ten blows Billy had delivered with his fists. When he hit me the first time I thought for an instant my horse must have boogered and kicked me in the ribs.

I saw the cedar stay coming again—this time toward my face—but my arms were too weary to block it and my head too slow and out of control to dodge it.

CHAPTER 7

I HAD BEEN A lone wanderer all of my life, and as I lay semiconscious on my face in the grass my mind took me back to the place where all the years of wandering had begun, the banks of the

Concho River. I was a little boy again, frightened and wondering why my mother had left me alone and why she hadn't come back to take me in her arms and protect me from the unseen things lurking in the river bushes.

I tried and tried for what seemed like days—and probably was no more than an hour or so—to keep my eyes open and lift my head off the ground. By then I knew I wasn't a little boy wandering along the banks of the Concho River, but for a while I wasn't sure of where I was or what had happened. Then, slowly, as I was able to keep my eyes open for longer and longer periods of time, I began to remember it all.

Finally, I was able to push myself up onto my hands and knees and lift my head enough to look around. It was nearly dark, a cool breeze was blowing, and thunder was rumbling from dark clouds beyond the northern rim of the basin. My piggin' string had been cut into short pieces. The gate was closed, but it looked like the calf had been dragged back through it. The cedar stay Floyd had used on me was there, and my horse was gone.

What little I had in my stomach suddenly came up, followed by dry heaves for a while. Each time my stomach contracted, the ribs on my left side hurt so bad it was almost more than I could tolerate, but what other choice did I have? The ribs not only hurt when I threw up, they hurt every time I took a breath. My head hurt, too, something terrible, and blood had dried on my face. My mouth was bone dry—too dry to even spit out the taste of vomit and blood.

I reached for the cedar stay and used it to help myself onto my feet, then used it as a walking stick.

I'd walked no more than twenty or thirty painful steps when I got the dry heaves again and could have sworn that my ribs were going to come out my mouth. The heaves finally subsided and I straightened up and started walking toward the east, but after a few more steps they gripped me again and left me so weak I sank into the grass on my back and tried not to even breathe.

It was almost dark by then. The thunder was a constant rumble and lightning was dancing on the northern rim.

After a few minutes, I pulled myself up and started walking again. I wasn't far from the west end of Big Butte Mesa, and instead of trying to make it all the way home that night I decided to try to get to the little cabin on the bench.

I'd walk for a spell and then get the heaves and have to lay down for a while again. It got dark, but the flashes of lightning lit up the sky enough so I could see Big Butte Mesa and always knew where I was.

The wind hit just as I found the trail angling up

the side of the mesa to the bench. I was wishing it would start raining so I could lift my face toward the sky and let the rain wash away the dried blood and wet my tongue, but although there was plenty of lightning that night, no rain was to come with it.

In the flashes of lightning I could see the narrow trail angling up and wondered if I could ever make it to the bench, but somehow I did. I passed out and when I came to, it was daylight and I was lying on my back beside the pool of springwater at the foot of the rock wall.

I rolled over and crawled to the edge of the pool and dipped my face into it and washed my mouth out. That alone made me feel better, but as soon as I swallowed a little water I started feeling sick again. I couldn't face the prospect of throwing up anymore, so I lay back down and closed my eyes. I knew my body needed more time, and since I had shade and water and shelter I was more than content to let it have that time.

Sometime later, I'm not sure how long, the sound of someone yelling my name woke me from a restless sleep. I opened my eyes and sat up and saw Judith stepping to the ground from her horse. She was leading my horse.

"My god, Concho," she said softly as she knelt beside me and put her hand on my arm. "What in the world happened?"

"My horse fell on me," I muttered.

She stood up. "We've got to get you to a doctor!"

I shook my head.

"Then I'll get Dr. Hammons to come out here."

"No! I don't need a doctor . . . I'm okay."

"You don't look okay!"

"In a couple of days I'll be good as new. Where'd you find my horse?"

"Walking along the fence not far from the gate . . . Let's get you in the cabin."

I nodded and started climbing up the cedar stay. Judith reached around to help me, but when she touched my sore ribs I yelled out and sank back to the ground. I looked up at her and tried to smile. "Just a couple of sore ribs," I said.

When we got inside the cabin, Judith spread a blanket on top of the felt mattress and I gingerly lowered myself onto the bed and watched her as she put wood into the stove and began to heat water.

"You're staring at me, aren't you?" she said without looking at me. "I guess you think I look like a man."

She was wearing a white blouse and a pair of Levis, and the way the Levis fit they couldn't have been Sid's. The blouse was buttoned to the throat, fell over her breasts and the shirt tail was tucked into the narrow waistband of the Levis. I'd seen women wearing Levis before and always thought they lacked something, took away the woman's femininity, but with Judith in them I thought they lacked for nothing—nothing at all.

"You don't look like any man I've ever seen," I said.

"Then stop staring at me."

"Yes, ma'am," I said as I turned my eyes toward the ceiling.

"I thought maybe you'd left, but when I went to the barn and saw your things still in the tack room I knew you hadn't. How did your horse come to fall on you?"

"I was going to rope and brand that red-necked heifer in case she got across the fence."

She turned to face me. "And? Your horse stepped in a hole . . . or what?"

"Yeah."

"I guess you're lucky—you could have wound up like Sid."

"Yeah."

"The water'll be hot in a few minutes and I'll clean the blood off your face." She walked to the side of the bed and began unbuttoning my shirt. "Let's have a look at your side."

She unbuttoned my shirt, pulled the shirttail out of my waistband, and spread the shirt open. "Roll over on your side," she said as she put her warm hands on me. "My god, Concho! That looks like you've been hit with a stick!"

"Does it?" I asked.

"I don't think a horse fell on you."

"You're an expert on what a fallin' horse can do to a man's body?"

She straightened up and looked down at me. "I know what I see . . . and your hands look like you've been in a fight."

"Is that water hot yet?"

She turned and stepped to the stove and tested the water with a finger. "Hot enough." She picked up the pan of water, using a towel for a pot holder, set it on the floor beside the bed, and rolled her sleeves up past her elbows.

Then she dipped the towel into it and wrung it out.

"How'd you get that bruise on your arm?" I asked, looking at the two-inch blue spot on the back side of her forearm.

"I bumped it on the saddle horn," she said as she laid the warm towel over my face. "There, let that soften up the blood."

I felt her get off the bed and heard her moving around the cabin. "The coffee will be ready in a few minutes and I'll heat up this can of beans. This is my favorite place—it's so quiet and peaceful and pretty here. This is where we spent our wedding night . . . I've ridden up here a few times alone in the past couple of months—usually when Sid was either passed out or so drunk he was absolutely intolerable. But it's nice even alone. Sometimes I wish I could just move up here and go back down to the house during the day to wash and cook and clean, and then come back here and swim in the spring and lay beside it on a blanket in the sun."

I heard her walk back to the bed and stop beside it. She lifted the towel off my face and began to wipe away the softened blood. When she was finished she poured steaming water into the pan on the floor and leaned over me. "Let's get that shirt off so I can put a hot towel on your ribs." When that was done she put a hand on my shoulder and looked down at me. "Feel better?"

"Yes . . . ," I answered softly. And I did.

"Want some beans and coffee now?"

"No . . . just a drink of water."

She got up and brought me some cold water in a tin cup; I sat up and drank half of it. Then I lay back down, closed my eyes, and fell into a deep sleep.

When I woke up Judith was putting another warm towel on my ribs.

"Well, hello," she said. "I put some witch hazel in the water—that should help draw the soreness out—and I've got some petroleum jelly with carbolic acid in it that I'll put on that beat-up face."

"Where'd you get all that stuff?" I asked.

"I went back to the house and told Sid what happened."

"What's that smell?"

She leaned over my face and went to work on it.

"That's stew warming up on the stove. Hungry?"

"Starved—and thirsty," I said. "How long have I been asleep?"

"All afternoon—the sun's already going down. There, that ought to help that face. Now, let's see if the stew's hot." She walked to the stove and tasted the stew with a spoon. "Almost," she said. Then she poured water from a sweating pitcher on the table into a tin cup and carried it to me. "This is fresh out of the rock wall."

"Ah . . . good . . . ," I said after I turned the cup up and drank it dry.

"Want some more?"

Although it hurt my ribs, I sat up on the edge of the bed, put my shirt on, then stood up with the cup in my hands.

"What are you doing?"

"Trying to not let myself get too spoiled," I said as I slowly moved to the table. I sat down on one of the rickety cowhide-bottomed chairs and poured myself another cup of water from the pitcher. "A man like me can't let himself get used to such things."

She dished out two bowls full of steaming stew and sat them on the table. She then opened the oven door and pulled out a pan of cornbread and sat it on the table between us.

"Gosh," I said with a smile. "If I'd known I was going to get treated this good, I'd have let . . . some horse fall on me the day after I got here."

"What really happened to you, Concho?"

"Just like I told you," I said. "What really happened to your arm?"

She looked surprised. "My arm . . . ? I bumped it on the saddle horn, just like I said I did. What do you think happened to it?"

I looked at her and raised my eyebrows.

"You thought . . . you think Sid did it?"

I shrugged and put a spoonful of stew in my mouth.

"No." She shook her head. "It's not that way between Sid and me. I know you heard us arguing the other night, but it's usually not that way between us. Usually, there's . . . nothing between us anymore to speak of. I wash and cook and clean and putter in the yard and garden, feed the chickens and gather the eggs, and milk the cow while he sits and reads the Bible or sits and drinks—and that's about it."

"What did he say about your coming back up here?"

She shrugged. "He said, 'See if he'll stay and get the calves branded.'"

"I've already been here a lot longer than I was planning on," I said.

"He's really been worrying about getting the calves branded. It's hard for him to have all of this and not be able to take care of it himself." She sat up straight in the chair. "I guess I'd better get back and see about him. If I were you, I'd just stay here tonight. I've put your horse in the corral and I brought him some grain, so he'll be fine."

I nodded. "Yeah . . . I think I'll do that."

"I brought up some more towels and some soap and your razor and a clean change of clothes."

"Thanks," I said, "but I didn't have any clean clothes."

She smiled. "You do now."

"Thanks again."

"You're welcome. You know," she said as she pushed her chair back and stood up, "you could stay up here all the time if you wanted to. I mean . . . if you decide to stay and get the calves branded like Sid wants you to, you could just stay up here instead of in the barn. After all, it's not but what, a couple of miles at the most, back down to the house?"

We looked at each other a few seconds, then she walked to the door, stopped, and turned around. "You never did say . . . will you stay?" She was framed in the doorway, her slender body with its gentle curves silhouetted against the dusky light behind her.

"Because Sid wants me to?" I asked.

She said nothing for a moment. She bit her lip and looked down at the floor. Then she raised her head again and looked into my eyes. "Because I want you to," she said.

The evening crickets were chirping in the grass, birds were singing in the trees, and water from the spring was murmuring its way from the pool to the basin floor below.

I slowly nodded. "Up here," I said. "I'll stay up here . . . I'll come down some time tomorrow and get the rest of my things and some groceries and see Sid."

Judith nodded, then turned quickly and left.

CHAPTER 8

SID WAS SITTING on the porch when I went back down to the ranch the next afternoon. A bottle of whiskey sat beside him. I was feeling better than I had a right to expect; my ribs were still sore, but I could ride as long as I didn't get out of a trot.

"You look like hell," Sid said as I stopped at the foot of the porch stairs. "Judith said a horse fell on you . . . You were luckier than I was."

"Yeah," I agreed. "I was a lucky son of a gun."

"She said your ribs might be broke, but they must not be or you wouldn't be able to get on a horse."

"Or maybe I'm just a double-tough son of a bitch," I said.

"Well," he said, "if I had to bet one way or the other, I'd bet on 'em not being broken."

I grinned.

"What're you gonna do now?"

"Judith said you wanted me to stay and get the calves branded."

Sid nodded, and then leaned over, picked up the whiskey bottle sitting on the porch at his side, took off the cap, and shoved it toward me.

I shook my head.

"Too good to drink with me—or just too proud?"

"Neither—just don't want a drink right now. You go ahead."

"Yeah . . . I will," he said, and took a drink. "What the hell else can I do?"

"What the hell else do you want to do?"

"I want to get on one of those good Van horses and ride through those good Van cattle. And I'd like to rope one of those cold-blooded Shiner cows just to listen to her beller."

"But you sit here on the porch, instead."

"Goddammit, Concho," he said as he hit his legs with his hands, "these things won't work!"

"If I sat and nursed on a bottle all day long I don't expect mine would work worth a damn either."

The muscles were about to rip out of Sid's jaws he was clenching his teeth so hard. "Just go to hell!" he said. "Drinking's the only thing I can still do, and—"

"—and you're makin' a damn fine hand at it," I said. "I'll need some help with the brandin'."

"What?" He stopped long enough to take another pull from the bottle. "Why, I figured a double-tough, big-outfit cowpuncher like yourself could brand a little ol' place like this in a couple of hours without any help at all."

"I can help," Judith said from the other side of the screen door as she wiped flour from her hands with her apron.

Me and Sid both looked at her.

"Well . . . I can!" she insisted. "There's a lot of things I can't do around cattle, but how complicated can branding a calf be?"

"You'll cook for Concho and whoever he can find to help him," Sid said as he turned his attention away from her and back to me. "I used to neighbor with Bob Shiner. He even brought his whole crew over last spring, right after I got hurt, and branded my calves for me. Then he came back last fall and shipped for me. But I wouldn't let Little Bob help if he offered, which he's sure not about to do. You'd better go to town and—"

The screen door opened, and when Judith stepped onto the porch she did not look like a happy cook. "I'll cook *and* ride!" she said.

"A branding crew's no place for a woman!" Sid said.

"Why not?"

"Because you've got eight or ten men who'll need to be relieving themselves, and there'll be bulls smellin' of cows and rearin' up on 'em and—and it's just no place for a woman, Judith! Good god!"

Judith wheeled around, jerked the screen door

open as wide as the spring would let it, went back inside, letting the door slam shut behind her. I looked down at the porch floor and grinned. Then I looked back at Sid. "When you feel like it," he said, "go to town and see who you can find to help. Tell 'em I'll pay two dollars a day and feed 'em. I can mount a couple of 'em, but I can't mount the whole crew, not with twelve head of saddle horses. You ought to be able to put a crew together for that kind of money. When do you think you'll feel like starting?"

"I'll go to town the day after tomorrow and get some help," I said. "I'll try to start work the next morning. If I can find enough help, I'll brand the west pasture outside and bring the east pasture up here to the pens."

Sid nodded. "I want to vaccinate the calves for black leg—you can get the vaccine from Grady Vinson at the mercantile and charge it to me."

"Okay . . . How many doses do you think I'll need?"

"I've got two hundred ninety-seven cows—or had that many. God knows how many I've got now."

"What about the dries?" I asked.

"Cut 'em out and leave 'em in the shipping trap," he said.

I nodded. "I'm going to stay up at the camp—"

"That's Dripping Springs," he said.

"Okay . . . I'm going to stay at Dripping

Springs. I'll take my bedroll and things up there today. The crew'll probably just stay in the barn."

"Are you still working for nothing?" Sid asked.

"Hell no," I said.

"What's the matter—lost that pride already?"

"No," I said, "I just figured you'd learned your lesson about pullin' that bullshit on me."

Sid looked at me. "You know, I hate to agree with anything Little Bob Shiner says, but maybe he was right about you."

I grinned and walked back out to my horse.

A large bank of thunderclouds built up in the west again late that afternoon, and this time they had more than just thunder and lightning in them. I put one of the cowhide-bottomed chairs out on the porch so I could watch the rain while day gave way to night. Usually, I could just sit and let myself enjoy the rain and the coolness, but that night I couldn't keep myself from thinking. First, about Malcolm Floyd. I never pictured myself as a fighter, but neither could I picture myself leaving the basin before seeing him again, not that I looked forward to that meeting with any great deal of enthusiasm. It was just something that I knew I had to do, like getting on a horse that's already stuck your head in the dirt once on a cold morning and can probably do it again. You might not really want to cheek him up and get back on, but then again you never really consider not doing it.

Then I thought a little about Sid too, but not much.

Sitting there that night, watching it rain, watching the lightning light up the sky and the basin all the way to the south rim, and listening to the thunder roll and sometimes crackle, mostly what I thought of was Judith. I remembered how she looked the first time I saw her and the first time I saw her smile a few days later. And how lonesome she looked, standing on the porch in the moonlight with the house dark and quiet behind her. I thought of how her hands felt on me when she was doctoring me, and the way she looked at me sometimes—like when she was standing in the doorway of the cabin when she raised her head and bit her lip and said *she* wanted me to stay.

The next morning, though I sure didn't feel like it, I knew I'd better check the water gaps between Sid and Shiner. Just like I was afraid of, the first one I came to had the bottom two wires broken. It didn't take much to tie them back together and tie a rock on them to hold them down, but handling that rock was almost more than my ribs could tolerate. As soon as I was finished, I rolled a smoke and stretched out in the grass in the shade to smoke it, but had taken no more than one puff when my horse threw his head up and nickered.

My first thought was, god, if that's Malcolm

Floyd, I hope he hasn't found another cedar stay!

"Loafing on the job, huh?" Judith said with a smile as she and her horse came into view above the rim of the creek bank.

I looked up at her and grinned, surprised to see her—but in no way disappointed. "Absolutely," I said. "You didn't think I reached this lofty status in life by hard work alone, did you?"

She found a place where the creek bank sloped enough to ride her horse down to the creek bed. She was wearing Levis again and a white shirt. Her hair was pulled back and tied with a ribbon, and she had nothing on her head.

"What're you doing here?" I asked. "Besides checkin' up on the help."

"Sid said the rain probably washed out some water gaps, and I had a hunch you didn't have any more sense than to try to put them in by yourself."

"So you came to help?"

Judith nodded. "Sid said it'd be a shame to let the cattle get scattered again after just getting them all back home."

I nodded. "So, what do you know about water-gappin'?"

"Why do you men always think everything you do is too complicated for a woman? How complicated can putting in a water gap be? If the wires are broken you tie 'em together and tie a rock on 'em to hold 'em down."

I laughed.

"What's so funny?"

I pulled myself painfully to my feet, unhobbled my horse, and looked across my saddle seat at her. "You bring any gloves?"

"Of course I did," she said. "And some wire pliers."

"Then, boss lady," I said, "sounds like you're ready to go water-gappin'."

It was one of those hot and humid days that happen sometime right after a big summer rain when the air is heavy and full of mosquitoes, gnats, and deerflies, and there's not enough breeze to stir even the topmost leaves on the tallest cottonwood trees, much less enough to cool somebody trying to untangle three strands of barbed wire that have been rolled and wadded together in the bottom of a narrow wash that still has a foot of warm water in the bottom of it.

In just a few minutes, Judith's white shirt was reddish brown from the red sand and silt she'd been digging in, and wet with sweat.

"We'll need a rock big enough to hold all three of these wires down," I said as I started to tie a loop in one end of the broken top wire.

Judith looked up at me. Her hair had come down and the ribbon that had been sitting proudly at the back of her head was hanging on for dear life to a half-dozen strands of sweaty hair over one shoulder.

"I think that big one right over there—"

"I think I'm smart enough to pick out a rock by myself," she said as she started toward the bank, slogging through the water-soaked sand and silt in her bare feet.

In a few minutes she came struggling back with a round rock that was about twice as heavy as it needed to be and dropped it at the edge of the water. "That's sure a nice one all right," I said. "But—"

"But what?"

"But you can't tie a wire around a round rock and make it stay."

Judith looked at the rock and then at me. Then she wiped the sweat off her face with a shirtsleeve and started back toward the bank. I began to whistle and run the other end of the wire I'd been working on through the loop I'd just tied. "More complicated than you thought it'd be?" I yelled.

"No," she said as she struggled back with another rock—this time an oblong one. "I guess I just thought you'd be more help."

I smiled as I got the right stretch on the wire and tied it off. "Ordinarily, I would be," I said. "But, you know, I have this horrible rib wound to deal with. But if you want to go back to the house and—"

"Not on your life!" she said as she dropped the rock about two inches from my bare toes.

I shot a quick glance at her and frowned and

started to tell her she ought to be more careful, but the way she was smiling at me I could tell she'd dropped the rock right where she meant to. So I just smiled back at her and proceeded to tie a wire around it without saying anything.

By the middle of the afternoon we'd been to about a half-dozen water gaps and had had to do at least a little work on all of them even if it was nothing more than to tie a rock on them. One had been completely washed out, just like the first one, but it wasn't any bigger than that one had been either. Luckily, I'd had enough sense to leave a little wire at every gap when I was fixing the fence after I first got there, so if we needed some it was there.

"I almost hate to look at this one," I said as we rode our sweated-out horses to the top of a ridge overlooking Smokey Hill Creek, one of the widest creeks the fence line crossed. It was right in the hottest part of a day that had started out hot. I was hot and tired and hungry, and although my ribs might not have been hurting as bad as I'd been letting on, they did hurt plenty. As for Judith, she had proven her point—water-gapping is as uncomplicated as it is unpleasant, hard work. She had proven that point to herself, but she had also proven to me that she had more grit and staying power than I'd suspected.

"Damn," I heard her whisper when we topped the ridge and looked down on the creek. If she hadn't been there I'd have made that word sound like a Sunday School lesson. The creek bed right there was a quarter mile wide and for at least half of that distance the fence was gone, posts and all. And this one was not a three-wire water gap but a four-wire one. I'd let myself hope that we'd see that some Shiner hands on the other side of the fence had already put it in, but since they hadn't been to any of the other gaps we'd put in, I guess it was silly to think they'd put in the biggest one.

Neither of us said anything else as we rode to the creek bank, hobbled the horses, and pulled off our boots.

After we'd dug out and untangled and got all the silt and trash off the wires and dug seven cedar posts out of the sand, Judith looked at me through the sweaty hair hanging over her face and said, "How do we dig the holes?"

I held up my hands and looked at them. "With these—in places the sand'll be so boggy we can work the posts down into it without diggin'."

"I'm wrung out," I said more than two hours later when we were finally sitting in the sand and pulling our boots on.

"You mean we're already through? And here I am, fresh as a daisy," Judith said.

"Yeah," I said "you look it, too. But we're *not* through . . . there's not any more big ones, but there's three or four more little ones along the south fence." I stood up and unhobbled my horse. "I can't wait to get back to Drippin' Springs and jump in that cool water. Sid's sure gettin' his money's worth today."

"At least *you're* getting paid," Judith said as she pulled the hobbles off her horse's forelegs.

"Yeah," I said and laughed. "And I don't have to sleep with him either."

That seemed to strike a sour note with her. "That's none of your business," she said.

I got on my horse. "I know . . . I just said it without thinking."

"Really, without thinking?" she asked.

I fiddled with my bridle reins a few seconds and looked down at my saddle. Then I raised my head and looked at her.

Judith looked at me a few seconds, then rode past me without saying anything else.

We didn't talk as we rode to the next water gap, and spoke very little as we fixed it, and that only about the business at hand.

The same with the next water gap.

And the silence held with the next one and the one after that, the last one. And it held all the way up the trail to the bench and Drippin' Springs, where we got off at the edge of the pool in the shade of the rock wall and let the horses water while we knelt beside them. Judith rolled her sleeves up and washed the dried sand off her hands and arms. Then she cupped water in her hands and washed her face while I took off my hat and dunked my head into the cool water.

Judith stood up. "Oh . . . that felt good," she said.

"Yeah," I said from my hands and knees as I held my head over the pool and let the water drip from it. "The best part about water-gappin' on a day like this is gettin' back to camp."

It was quiet for a little while, except for birds singing in the trees and the sound of water dripping into the pool on one end and running out of it in a narrow stream on the other. Judith pulled her boots off and sat in the sand at the edge of the pool and put her feet into the water. "Oh, Concho," she said, "pull your boots off. This feels so good."

"Cowboys don't pull their boots off and stick their feet in cool water!" I said as I ducked my head again.

"No . . . they just blubber in it like a dog."

"That's right. If you weren't here I'd jump in like a dog, too, and just lay in it with nothing but my head out of the water."

She stood up and moved behind me—I thought to put on her boots.

"Don't let me stop you," she said as she put her foot on my rump and shoved so hard I landed headfirst in the pool like a hundred-and-seventy-pound awkward frog.

The pool got deep fast, and by the time I'd

thrashed around, got my head up so I wouldn't drown, turned myself over and got my feet underneath me instead of behind me, I was already standing in waist-deep water.

I blew the water off my lips and mustache and wiped my dripping hair back. I wasn't any more than three feet from the edge, but it was a steep slope and I slipped down with the first step I took toward it. I stood up again and held a hand toward Judith for help. She smiled at me from between the horses and shook her head.

I crawled out of the water and onto the bank like a water dog. Judith tried to get on her horse, but my sloshing boots coming toward him boogered him and made him spin away from her.

"Don't, Concho!" she said as she tried to run past me. I cut her off in that direction and watched her back toward the rock wall with her hands out in front of her.

I raised my eyebrows and smiled.

"Concho . . . I'm sorry. It was just too tempting."

"I understand," I said.

"I thought it would feel good," she said.

"It did," I said as I started slowly toward her.

"Concho . . . Please!" she said, laughing. "Don't forget about your ribs. Remember how sore they are? Why you said they were too sore to even pick up a twenty-pound rock! I—I thought the cold water would make them feel better."

"It did," I said, laughing and crouching a little as I kept moving toward her.

She was only a few feet in front of the rock now and less than a foot from where the water coming from it would fall on her.

She stood up straight and put her hands on her hips. "Now, Concho—stop! I can't go home with my clothes all wet. What will Sid think?"

I shrugged and stopped for a moment. "You shoulda thought about that two minutes ago. You're going in that water, Judith—you'd just as well get ready for it. There's only one way you're not going to get your clothes wet."

"And how is that?" she asked.

"Take 'em off," I answered.

"I'm sure you think I won't."

"I'm sure you're right."

"I might surprise you, you know."

"You might, but if you're going to, you'd better get started."

She looked at me with a strange smile on her face for a few seconds, with a different sparkle in her green eyes from what I'd seen before. But then she sighed, raised her arms, and said, "All right . . . here. Go ahead and get it over with if that will make you feel better."

"That won't work either," I said as I walked up to her and picked her up in my arms. I suppose my ribs were bound to have been hurting, but if they were, no pain registered in my brain. All that

110

registered with me, and not only in my brain, was the way she felt in my arms, the way her right breast was pressed against my chest, and how close my face was to hers.

"You really don't think I'll do it, do you?" I said, standing sideways at the edge of the water as I held her.

"If that's the kind of man you are, then—"

"It is," I said as I turned and opened my arms, trying to throw her as far into the water as possible, but at the last moment her right hand came behind my neck.

We hit the water with one big splash. My head went under, and water rushed into my nose. I came up spitting and coughing while Judith stood in waist-deep water and laughed. Her hair wasn't even wet—but it was ten seconds later, after I lunged at her, tackled her, and we both went under.

We came up spitting and laughing together. She flung her dripping hair back and sunk until only her head was out of the water. "Oh . . . I'm still mad at you—but this does feel good. This is deeper than you'd think. It's over your head—did you know that?"

"No," I said. "This is the first time I've ever been in it."

"Not me. I've been swimming in it a few times. This is the first time I've ever been in it with my clothes on, though."

"I gave you a chance to take 'em off," I said.

"Now, you didn't really think I would, did you?" she said as she drew her arms back and forth through the water.

"No," I said.

She laughed again. "Just playing in the water like this is a big step for old Prudith Judith, believe me."

"Prudith Judith?"

"Yes . . . that's what some people back home call me—not to my face, of course."

"Where's home?"

"Brawley, Minnesota—where I taught school."

"A schoolteacher?"

"That's right, a schoolmarm." She flung her hair back again and laughed. "I'll bet you thought I had some tongue-clicking, eyebrow-raising past, didn't you?"

"Of course not."

"You're not a very good liar," she said. "Of course you did. What other kind of woman would be a mail-order bride . . . right? I think even Sid thinks I have some kind of scandalous past."

"I guess I just never pictured you as a schoolteacher, that's all," I said.

"Well, I was—Miss Prim and Proper, who never caused a single tongue to click or eyebrow to rise in her entire life."

"I didn't know we had so much in common," I said.

She looked at me with teasing eyes. "Uh-huh . . . sure, Concho. But that's okay—sometimes I wish I had the nerve to do something I shouldn't. You know just do it! I've always been the good girl, always done what was expected of me. I always did what mother and daddy expected of me, and after they died, I always did what Aunt Lela Mae expected of me, and after that it was the Brawley County school board and on and on—*always* doing the right thing, the proper thing, the *expected* thing.

"When I got up the courage to come out here— and where I got it I haven't the slightest idea—I thought everything would be different. I was going to marry a handsome western rancher and there was going to be romance and—and everything I'd never had before. But guess what? Nothing's really changed. Now I do what Sid expects me to. I wash and clean and cook and wait on him and don't even get a thank-you for it. Sid expects me to do it. And what do I do? I do it. I guess I've thought that if I did enough for him, he'd love me again—if he ever did, that is."

"What kind of man was he?" I asked. "I mean, before he got crippled."

"Oh . . ." She seemed to be lost for a few seconds. ". . . he was wonderful. Our courtship was short—only three weeks—and then, of course, we'd only been married two weeks to the day when the accident happened. But those five weeks were the best five weeks of my life. Everything was even better than I'd dared hope it would be—Sid was kind and gentle and romantic and we were so much in love and talking about how many kids we would have. I told him we'd better get busy because I wasn't a young woman anymore. Of course, we were just getting to know each other and everything was still new. He was on his best behavior"—she looked at me and smiled—"but of course so was I. I guess the memory of those five weeks was enough to keep me holding on for a long time and hoping—"

"—that he'd get better?"

"Get better? Of course. But it's that closeness we had that I miss more than anything . . . His getting crippled didn't have to stop that, but . . ."

"But it did, huh?"

"Yes. If we ever touch at all now it's strictly by accident. But, you know, even if he was to touch me on purpose now I'm not sure what I'd do."

"Let me see . . . ," I heard a man's voice say, "I'm guessing that you either lost your wire pliers and you two was divin' for 'em, or else you was practicing your water-gappin'."

I turned around in the water and saw Shorty sitting on a horse with his forearms resting on the saddle horn. He was grinning.

"Hi, Shorty," I said. "This is . . . this is Mrs. Van."

Shorty touched his hat. "Glad to meetcha, ma'am."

"Yes . . . thank you," Judith said, and stepped

out of the water up onto the bank with her arms crossed in front of her breasts.

"Shorty . . . ," I said "get a towel out of the cabin, will you?"

"Sure enough," he said as he reined his horse around and trotted to the front of the cabin.

"My god!" Judith said as I stepped out of the water.

"It's okay," I said. "After all, we weren't doing anything—not really."

She rolled her eyes and smiled. "Shh . . . ," she said. "Here he comes." She turned to face the rock wall so her back would be to both me and Shorty.

Then she turned her head and looked over her shoulder at me one last time, looked into my eyes, and smiled and whispered, "It was a good day, Concho. The best I've had in a long time."

"Tell Sid I'll try to start brandin' the day after tomorrow. I'd plan on feeding at least seven or eight men for breakfast, if I were you."

CHAPTER 9

SHORTY WAS SITTING on his horse and grinning after Judith had put on her boots, got on her horse, and rode off the bench. "Most people would put their horse up and pull off their boots before they got in the water," he said.

"I guess most would," I said. "What're you doing here?"

"Sid . . . that's *Mister* Van—you know, the crippled guy with the crutches—said you and Mrs. Van were out water-gappin', but he said you'd been staying up here so I came on up to wait till you got back from doin' all that hard work in the hot sun."

"We just got through," I said.

"It must've been awful tough work. I'm glad to see you held up to it so good, though. And Mrs. Van too—she seemed to 've come through it in pretty good shape herself. As a matter of fact, I'd say she came through it in *damn* fine shape, all things considered, of course."

"You're on the wrong side of the fence, aren't you?"

"I quit Shiner's this morning—came to see if you were still here or had left without me."

"Why would you think I'd do that?" I asked.

"Billy Wright. By the looks of your face, maybe he wasn't lyin'."

"This face is a compliment to the stayin' power of a cedar stay in Malcolm Floyd's hands, not to anything Billy Wright did."

"He forgot to mention that," Shorty said.

"I bet he did."

"He just said him and Malcolm caught you tryin' to steal a calf. Then he laughed and said he figured you were already across the border by now. And hell, I think we should be. You ready?"

"Not quite," I said.

"You know, you're gonna find this strange as hell, but somehow or other I just had a feeling that's what you were goin' to say—I guess it had something to do with the way you and . . . what's her name?"

"Judith," I said.

"Yeah. I guess it had something to do with the way you and Judith were gigglin' and . . ."

"We weren't gigglin'," I said. "Let's unsaddle our horses and put 'em in the pen. Then I'll make some coffee and fix us something to eat."

"Fish?"

I looked at him. "Whatta you mean—fish?"

"I mean, with all that water in your boots, you're bound to have a fish or two in each one. I thought we might have 'em for supper."

I stuck my hat over my wet hair and sloshed past him, leading my horse toward the corral.

"I'm sorry, Concho," he said with a snicker as he rode behind me. "I guess I said the wrong thing—hell, frog legs'll be fine if that's what you and Mrs. Van were seinin' for."

"Just go to hell, Shorty," I said.

"Damn, but a long day of water-gappin' in the hot sun makes a man sour, don't it?"

"Yeah, it does," I said. "It makes me outa sorts, and always will. Maybe you oughta remember that."

"Outa snor . . . What did you say it makes you out of?"

"Sorts . . . It makes me outa sorts! You gettin' deaf?"

"No, I ain't gettin' deaf," Shorty said as he stepped off his horse and began loosening his latigo. "I just thought you said 'outa snorts,' and I was going to say you probably used all of 'em snortin' in your water-gappin' partner's flank."

"I wasn't snortin' in anybody's flank," I said.

"Yeah . . . unh-huh . . . and ducks don't float either. But hell, I would, too—I mean how many times do men like us get to snort in the flank of a woman like her? Huh?"

"Happens to me all the time," I said as I laid my saddle on the ground and turned the wet saddle blankets wet-side up over it.

"Unh-huh . . . You're full of shit as a Christmas turkey, too."

"I told Sid I'd stay a few days and get his calves branded for him," I told Shorty when we were eating. "You can help, too."

"What about Malcolm Floyd—you gonna let him splinter-up a cedar stay on you and—?"

"It was a damn good stay. It didn't splinter a bit," I said. "Are you gonna help me get Sid's calves branded?"

"I'd rather go with the water-gappin' crew."

"Dammit, Shorty," I said. "Are you gonna keep that up all night?"

"No . . . I plan on going to sleep in a couple of

hours. Why don't you just tell me all the sordid details and then I'll probably shut up."

"There's no sordid details to tell. We *had* been water-gappin' all day, and we were hot and tired when we got here." I shrugged. "We got to horsing around and wound up dunking each other in the spring—that's all!"

"Well, damn, Concho—you don't have to get mad. Hell, do you think I'd hold it against you? She's a hell of a good-lookin' woman! A hell of a lot better lookin' than that wife old Jimbo Bonner had. What was her name?"

"Hell, I don't know," I said. "I don't know Jimbo Bonner."

"Yeah, you do—he had that outfit along the Snake River."

I shook my head. "Never worked there."

"You didn't? I thought you were there when I was. You'd have remembered it, though, if you had been. Jimbo got 'im a wife out of Boise who never could remember to keep her skirts down— she was horsin' around *all* the time. Can't remember what her name was, though . . . Pam! That was it—Quiverin' Ham Pam we called her. Used to sneak out to the bunkhouse after old Jimbo'd gone to bed."

"Well . . . god, Shorty!" I said. "Judith's not like that. Hell, she was a schoolteacher and sung in the choir! This is a rough time for her."

"And being the kind soul you are, you intend to

119

make it a little smoother, huh? Well, hell, Concho, like I said—I don't blame you. After all, it's not your fault Sid's crippled, is it? And men like us, we have to take our pleasure where we find it, don't we?"

I shrugged and didn't say anything.

"Don't we?"

"I guess so. Are you goin' to help get Sid's calves branded?"

"Yeah, I'll help you," he answered. "What about Floyd?"

"I don't think he'd be much help."

"You know what I mean. I just figured you wanted to see him again before we left."

"Oh, yeah . . . hell, yeah," I said. "I'm just dyin' to see him again and get another good tunin'-up with a cedar stay."

"I'm beginnin' to think another tunin'-up might not hurt you a bit."

"Yeah," I said, "I think you might be right— maybe I oughta just go find old Malcolm right now."

That night after dark when we were lying on our blankets, Shorty said, "What'd we ever do to the cowpunchin' gods that we both wound up down here with these no-savvy bastards anyway?"

I shrugged. "I don't know—maybe it was because we never really appreciated any of the good outfits we've been on."

"Who else you got to help us brand?"

"Just you and me so far. I'll go to town tomorrow and see who else I can find."

"Okay. So what's the deal between you and Sid's wife? I mean really."

"Nothing, Shorty! She's *not* like that other woman you were talkin' about."

"Damn . . . I'm sorry. But you know, men like us . . ."

"Shorty," I said, "just go to sleep, will you?"

"Yeah," he said, and in a few minutes I could hear him snoring softly.

I don't know how long it was before I finally went to sleep, but it was a long time. I got up once and walked outside to the spring again in the moonlight. The night birds were singing and coyotes were yipping in the distance. Somewhere, not far from the foot of the bench, a cow bawled twice for her calf, probably because she'd seen a coyote sneaking around. The pool of water was quiet and still except for the water running into and out of it . . . but in my mind I could still see Judith in it, slinging her wet hair back and laughing. She said it had been a good day, and it had been, but there's a bad thing to certain good days that drifting men know only too well—when they're over and you're thinking about them in the moonlight afterward, they leave you so lonesome you almost wish they'd never happened.

• • •

It was still and pretty the next morning, and at least for a basin stuck down between two high rims, it was cool too. The air was so clear that I heard hammering coming from town two miles before I got there. That hammering was coming from the barn going up next to Vinson's Mercantile in the middle of town.

I tied my horse up in front of the store and went inside. A couple of women were looking at the dresses hanging on a rack, and a man was fiddling with some harness hanging on the wall. "Are you Grady Vinson?" I asked him.

"No," he said. "He's in the back with someone. He'll return in a minute."

I waited next to the counter. In a couple of minutes three men came through the door that led to the back of the mercantile—a man in a clerk's apron, Robert Shiner, and Malcolm Floyd.

"Good morning," the man in the apron said.

I looked at Floyd for a few seconds, then looked at the man in the apron. "Are you Grady Vinson?"

"Yes, sir," he said.

"I need to get three hundred doses of black leg and charge it to Sid Van."

"Why sure," he said, turning around to open the glass-covered cabinet behind him. "Do you need syringes too?"

"Sid didn't say, but I probably oughta have some, I guess—maybe a half dozen."

"All right," Grady Vinson said as he was putting the vaccine and syringes into a small box. "You must be Sid's new hand—Concho Smith."

"Yeah," I said.

Vinson turned around, sat the box on top of the counter, and stuck his hand toward me. "I've heard about you, Mr. Smith . . . glad to meet you."

I shook Vinson's hand. "This is Robert Shiner and Malcolm Floyd. Robert owns—"

"We've met," I said. I looked at them and smiled. "How're you fellers doing?" They looked at me and didn't say anything. "How's your hands, Malcolm? Got any splinters in 'em?"

"I'm glad Sid's finally got somebody who can take care of that place for him," Vinson said, sliding the box across the counter toward me. "Here you go—tell Sid I said hello."

"I will," I said. "Know anybody that I can get to help with the branding?"

"No," he said, "not right offhand. Most of the men around here are already working." He turned his head toward Shiner and Floyd. "Do ya'll know of anybody?"

"Not a soul," Shiner said.

"I guess you and Mrs. Van will have to brand 'em by yourselves," Floyd said.

"I already got one good hand," I said. "I think you know him—Shorty Wayman."

Shiner bristled.

"We know him," Floyd said. "He might be all right on a little outfit like Sid's."

I smiled again, picked up the box, thanked Grady Vinson, and walked toward the door.

"Good luck in finding any help," Floyd said. "You might try the Mex'can shanties on the south side of town—that's where we get our fencers."

We were eating breakfast around the oak table two hours before daylight the next morning in Sid's house—Sid, me and Shorty, and two Mexican brothers about fourteen years old, Juan and Pablo Garcia.

"Where's the rest of 'em?" Sid asked.

"This is it," I said as I put some wild plum jelly on a biscuit.

"You call this a branding crew?"

"Maybe you'd rather ask Robert Shiner real nice if he'd send some men over."

"That'll be a cold day in hell," Sid said.

Judith took off her apron. "I'm helping, too."

Sid looked at her. "You know what I told you."

"Yes, I know *exactly* what you told me—a crew of eight or ten men is no place for a woman. Do you see eight or ten men, Sid? I proved I can water-gap . . . and I can help brand too!"

Sid looked at me, and I shrugged.

"Who's gonna cook dinner?" Sid asked.

"I will," she said. "I'll fix dinner when we get back—while the men rest."

Sid looked at me again, and again I shrugged. Then he looked at Juan and Pablo. "You boys ever flanked calves before?"

Juan and Pablo looked at each other, then looked at Sid. "No savvy," Juan said.

"Good god," Sid said, and looked at me. "How are you gonna brand the west pasture outside?"

"We're not," I said. "We'll throw it into the east pasture this mornin'. Tomorrow we'll bring everything to the shipping trap, cut out the dries, and throw 'em in the horse pasture. Then we'll brand everything the next day."

"Got it all figured out, don't you."

"What's a highly paid cow boss for?" I asked.

"Well, Mister Highly Paid Cow Boss, did you think our lives would ever come down to this?" Shorty asked as we trotted ahead of the rest of the "crew" in the predawn light. "I mean, when we first went up the trail together with those three thousand head of longhorns for Elliot and there wasn't a fence from Pecos to Purgatory, did you imagine that one day we'd be trottin' to the back side of a little ol' pasture to gather it with two Mex'can kids and a woman?"

"Life does have its twists and turns," I agreed.

When we got to within a half mile of the northwest corner of the west pasture, I stopped on top of a hill. By then it was light enough to see. "Judith," I said, "you see the corner down there?"

"I see it," she answered.

"You drop off here, and stay close enough to the north fence so you can see it. We're gonna take everything to that gate I threw back—the one where you got in the cactus."

She was listening closely and nodding.

"Every chance you get, top out on a hill and see if you can see how the drive's goin', see whether you need to speed up or slow down. We're going to be quite a ways apart, but do the best you can."

"Do you think I'd do anything else?" she asked.

Shorty looked at me and smiled.

"No . . . I don't think you would," I said. "Just take care of all the country between you and Juan, and try not to get ahead or behind. It's going to be quite a while before I get around the outside, so you may have a pretty good wait. That gate was down when I got here, so some of these old cows are used to going back and forth through it."

After we'd gone about a mile and a half down the west fence, I stopped and tried to tell Juan what was going on, then left him on top of a little knoll, smiling and nodding.

Three hills later, I dropped Shorty off and then Pablo, telling him—or trying to—to stay between me and Shorty and that he couldn't head straight toward the gate, but would have to flank me up around the outside.

I left Pablo smiling and nodding, too, and that was the last time I saw him till we were almost at the gate. Shorty had to flank me up and gather all the country between me and Juan, which turned out to be quite a bit because Juan saw Judith driving about twenty head of cows down the north fence and rode over to help her and there he stayed.

It wasn't that Sid's cows were wild, it was just that as soon as me or Shorty started one little bunch and then had to leave them to start some more a half mile or more away, they would stop. So it was back and forth, back and forth, whipping Van cows on the butt with a doubled catch rope and yelling and trying every way in the world to stir them up enough so they would go on without someone right behind them all the time. There were a handful wild enough to go on, but the rest would stop as soon as we left them.

About five hours later, when me and Shorty had gathered about a hundred and fifty head of cows with their calves and finally got them pushed to within a half mile of the gate, Juan and Pablo decided that if they didn't help us slow-moving gringos we might not ever get through. Our horses were used up, and we were cussing those no-driving Van cows and any- and everyone who had ever saddled a horse in the basin.

When we had pushed the last of the cows through the gate and I got off to shut it, Judith said, "That was even easier than I thought it would be, Concho. And you said it would be a long way between me and Juan, but it wasn't. I never even had to ride to the top of a hill to see him."

I just stood beside my horse for a minute and looked at her and nodded. "Shows you how much I know, don't it."

CHAPTER 10

THAT NIGHT AT supper I said, "I think we'll just gather half of the east pasture tomorrow and—"

"How come?" Sid asked.

"Because we're a little shorthanded and those old cows are the most no-drivin' things I've ever—"

"The hell they are!" he said.

"Me and Juan didn't have any trouble driving ours," Judith said.

"You got me there," I said. "But it's awful hot, and we're going to have twice as many head tomorrow and—"

"And if they try to run off . . . ," Shorty said, glancing at me and winking.

"They're pretty fat—if they try to run off you're liable to melt the taler in one of 'em," Sid said.

"Or gall a horse," Shorty added.

"Maybe you'd better take an extra day, Concho," Sid said. "What's one more day, anyway? You can gather half of 'em tomorrow and put 'em in the shipping trap."

"I'm surprised you didn't think of that,

Concho," Shorty said, "being the highly paid cow boss you are."

The next day went better than the first one had, mainly because me and Shorty only had half as much country to gather.

The third day we gathered the other half of the east pasture and shoved them and the ones we'd gathered the day before into a corner of the shipping trap.

I explained to Juan the best I could about holding up the cuts, and then with Shorty, Judith, and Pablo holding the herd in the corner I rode in to start cutting out the dry cows.

There was a dry standing at the edge of the herd right in front of Judith. "Let 'er out," I said as I pushed the cow toward her.

As soon as I rode back into the herd I saw another one with a handful of wet cows just to the right of Judith. I got between the cows and the herd and was going to let the wet cows work themselves out, but Judith didn't turn them back. Instead, she just sat there on her horse and watched them all walk out.

I trotted around them and pushed the whole works back into the herd without saying anything to Judith. The dry was at the back of the handful and I sliced her off and turned her back toward the cuts by myself.

The very same thing happened a few minutes later—Judith let a whole handful of wet cows out with the dry I was after, and I had to trot around the whole works and bring them all back into the herd and start over.

This time I pushed them toward Shorty, and he turned the wet cows the dry was with back until the dry was standing there by herself. Then Shorty moved over and I drove her out of the herd.

I cut two or three more out to Shorty without a hitch, then I wound up with three wets and a dry in front of Judith again. I figured she'd watched Shorty enough to know what to do.

But she just sat there and let all of them walk out of the herd—again.

I trotted around them, brought them all back, and started over—again.

And once more, Judith sat there while they started walking out.

"Turn the bitches back!" I said.

She moved over in front of them, and when they turned back I kept the dry from going back to the herd with the rest and boogered her toward the cuts.

The next one I cut to out where Shorty was, and when I started back into the herd he said, "There's something you don't see ever'day."

I stopped my horse and turned around and looked at him.

"What?"

"A cowhand leavin' the herd and goin' to the house in tears."

"What?"

He pointed behind him with a thumb, and sure enough, Judith was walking her horse past the cuts, headed in the direction of the house.

"Judith?" I said when I trotted up beside her. "Where're you goin'? Are you cryin'?"

She wasn't exactly crying then, but her face was wet, and I knew it wasn't from sweat. "You didn't have to cuss me!" she said, looking straight ahead and keeping her horse in a walk.

"I didn't cuss you!"

"You did! Cussed *and* yelled! . . . 'Turn the bitches back!'"

"Okay . . . I'm sorry. Will you stop?"

She pulled her horse up and looked at me.

"I apologize," I said, "but I can't cut anything out if you don't turn 'em back."

"But the first time you said, 'Let her out!'."

"But that was a dry by herself. When somebody brings several toward you, you've got to turn 'em all back and let him hold the one he wants."

"I'm supposed to know that?"

"I guess not," I said.

"Wouldn't it have been nicer if you'd told me that to begin with instead of yelling and cussing?"

"Absolutely," I said, nodding. "You're right. It would've been a *lot* nicer. Now let's go back to the herd, okay?"

She looked at me a minute. Then she rolled her eyes and smiled. "Maybe I was a little too

131

sensitive . . . but, 'Turn the bitches back!'? Really, Concho!"

I couldn't help but laugh then, and before we got back to the herd we were both laughing.

"This ain't as easy as it looks," I said to Shorty when I got back to the herd and rode up to him.

"I always admired a cow boss who—" he started.

"Get in there and whittle out the rest of those dries and shut up," I said.

Before we started branding the next day, me and Shorty tried to show Juan and Pablo how to flank calves when they were dragged to the fire by the hocks—how one of them should pull on the rope while the other jerked the tail, how to make the calves fall with their left sides up, and how to hold their hind legs and head so they couldn't get up while they were being worked.

Sid came out to the corrals on his crutches and said that if we could pile the wood close enough he could keep the fire burning for us.

When the irons were hot, I looked at Judith's sunburned face and said, "You can brand—I'll show you how when Shorty drags the first calf to the fire."

The first two calves Shorty roped by the hocks and dragged next to the fire both got away from the boys before they were ever on the ground. I schooled them some more, and they got the third calf down, but he jerked his hind legs free, kicked both boys unmercifully, and trotted back into the herd.

"Well," I said to Judith as we stood beside the fire, our shoulders touching, "I mean I'll show you how when the first calf Shorty drags to the fire is on the ground long enough to brand—which should be sometime before noon anyway."

At last the boys got a calf on the ground and were holding him right. "Bueno, boys!" I said as I picked up a branding iron and handed it to Judith.

"Remember, the open part of the brand goes toward the backbone." I put my foot in the calf's flank and my hands over Judith's on the branding iron. "When you put the iron on, do it hard enough so it won't slip and blotch the brand. If you don't hold it on long enough it won't burn through the hair, and if you hold it on too long it'll burn through the hide. When you lift the iron off, the brand should be shiny and not dull."

I stuck the iron to the calf's hip and branding smoke boiled up. Judith stepped back, coughing and holding her eyes.

I lifted the iron, looked at the brand, and handed the iron back to Sid to put in the fire.

"I forgot to tell you," I said to Judith with a grin as I took the knife from the sheath sewn onto my chap leg, "that sometimes the smoke's pretty bad."

"Thanks a lot," she said as she wiped tears from her eyes and watched as I castrated, earmarked, and vaccinated the calf.

When the next calf was on the ground, Sid handed Judith another branding iron. When she lifted the iron off the calf she looked at me. "A little more," I said.

When she lifted the iron again I nodded my head, and when I raised my eyes to look at her she was smiling. "I just branded my first calf," she said.

Sid took the branding iron from her and stuck it back into the fire. Then I saw him look at Judith and then at me.

"How're you doin'?" I asked.

"Hell, I'm okay," he answered, looking straight ahead, and in a couple of seconds added, "It just hurts a little bit."

"Your legs or your back or what?"

"No"—he shook his head a little—"just watching all this."

"I wouldn't mind watchin' about two hundred and seventy head of my own calves being branded," I said.

He raised his head and looked at me like I was crazy. "You know what I mean!" he said.

Left without anything to say, I watched Shorty double-hock a heifer, gracefully pivot his horse underneath the rope while he held the slack in the air, and start toward the fire.

After I earmarked and vaccinated the calf, I

looked at the brand Judith had just lifted the iron from. "See how dull it is?" I said. "It won't peel." I leaned over and ran my hand hard over the brand and the rest of the calf's hip and stood up again. "When there's a lot of dirt in the hair like that, you've got to knock it out—now try it again. Be sure to put the iron right back where it was."

Smoke rolled off the calf's hip as she put the hot iron on it again.

"Just right," I said when she lifted the iron and the smoke cleared enough to see the brand.

When Judith handed the iron to Sid I said to her, "If a calf really goes to squirmin', you'll probably have to lift the iron off until he stops. If it slips on the hide, the brand'll blotch."

"And that's bad?" she said.

I laughed. "Yeah—unless you want to steal the calf later, that's bad."

"I'll remember that," she said, and then walked away.

"I should be the one teaching her how to brand," Sid said.

I looked at him. "Yeah, but you never would have, would you? You wouldn't have let her come out here if you'd had a full crew."

"And you wouldn't either," he said. "Not if you had a full crew."

"You're probably right," I agreed.

"How'd the water-gappin' go the other day?"

"We got 'em all put in," I said. "And that big one across Smokey Hill Creek was plum out."

"Pretty hot, wasn't it?" he asked.

"Hotter 'n a by-god," I said. "But Judith's got a lot of heart."

He looked at me. "Is that right?"

"Yeah," I said as Shorty started toward the fire with another calf. "I'd like to have a string of horses that had that much heart."

Shorty was a hand with a rope, and just as soon as Juan and Pablo let one calf up he had another waiting for them. He roped most of them by both hocks, but one wild, stout bull calf kicked hard with both hind feet just as the rope was closing up on them and slipped his right hoof out of the loop. I'd told the boys that whenever they found themselves on the wrong side of the rope to never go around in front of the calf to get to the other side, but although they smiled and said they savvied, I don't think they savvied at all. Their cowboyese and my Spanish came together in very few places, and that particular set of instructions was not one of those places. Because when Shorty brought that wild bull calf to the fire by one hock, the first thing Pablo tried to do was to run around the front of him from the left, which did what it was almost guaranteed to do—caused the calf to turn back and start making a big circle on the end of rope.

I was sharpening my knife and not paying much

attention until it was too late. About all I had time to do was to yell, "Don't . . . Look out!" and grab for Sid.

The calf was kicking and trying to get back to the herd and away from Pablo, who was still trying to get around him. That meant the calf was making a fast circle to the right on the end of a right rope.

Sid and Judith were both close to the fire, and the only benefit they got from my yelling was that they got to see the rope a split second before it hit them.

Sid tried to duck in the hope that the rope would pass over him, but it didn't—it caught just enough of his back to send him and his crutches tumbling just before I could get to him, not that I could have done anything about the inevitable anyway.

If I hadn't been trying to get Sid out of the way, I could have dropped to the ground and let the rope pass over me, but instead I went tumbling to the ground with him.

Judith was closer to the calf—where the rope was lower—and tried to jump to let it pass underneath her. But the rope caught just enough of her heels to send them over her head.

Luckily, all three of us missed landing in the fire, but it was a darn good wipeout nonetheless.

By the time I looked up, Shorty had wheeled his horse around and dragged the calf back toward the herd so he wouldn't wipe us out on the second go-round. Judith was just getting up yelling, "Oh, god, Sid!"; Sid was lying face down in the dirt between us, quite a way from where his crutches had landed.

"Sid . . . are you okay?" Judith asked almost hysterically as I helped her carefully roll him over.

Sid blinked a few times, looked at Judith, then at me, and then back at her.

"Are you okay?" Judith asked again, the tears already forming in her eyes.

"You don't think this is the first time I've ever been wiped out around a brandin' fire, do you?" Then to me: "You should've told those boys not to ever get in front of a calf around a brandin' fire!"

"That's a hell of an idea, Sid!" I said. Then I looked at Judith. "Are you okay?"

"Yeah," she said. "I'm fine."

"Nice flip," I said.

She smiled big. "Thank you."

"Help me up and let's brand," Sid said.

It was dusty, and as the sun climbed higher in the sky the temperature rose until the corrals felt like an oven and sweat dripped from our foreheads and made white streaks down our dusty necks.

When Shorty's horse got tired, I would catch him another one from the remuda while the rest of the crew rested a few minutes and drank water from a metal dipper.

At a little after two, the last calf was trotting back into the herd, bawling for its mother and wringing its tail at the sting on its hip.

"I'd better go start dinner," Judith said, pushing the sweaty hair out of her dirty face. "Or do you need me out here some more?"

"No," I said. "Why don't you clean up and rest for a little while. We've got to push everything back into the shippin' trap and hold 'em up for a while. If dinner's not ready when we're done, we can wait."

She started toward the house. "Judith!" I said.

She stopped and turned back.

"You were good help."

She smiled. "Thank you," she said. "And you didn't have to cuss me a single time."

"Catch that little bay with the star on his forehead and one white hind sock," Sid said while I was getting a drink of water. Shorty was loosening the cinches on his horse to let him blow a minute, and Juan and Pablo had already gone to unhobble their horses.

"I don't need a fresh horse," I said. "Hell, all we're going to do is push 'em into the shipping trap and hold 'em on water a little while."

"I mean, catch the bay and put *my* saddle on him," he said.

I waited for him to laugh at his own joke, but he never did.

"What for?" I asked.

"So I can help you."

"Sid . . . I know it's hard to just have to watch while—"

"You don't know half as much as you think you do! Now, will you catch the bay for me?"

"Sid . . . Come on! You can't—"

"And how the hell do you know I can't?"

"How the hell do you know you can?"

"I don't! But if you'll catch the bay and put my saddle on him I'll find out . . . Or am I going to have to catch the son of a bitch and saddle him myself?"

"How come all of a sudden—?"

"The 'how comes' on this outfit are none of your goddamn business!" he said through clenched teeth. "You think you're so much better than everybody else because you've made the long trail drives and worked on big ranches, but look at you—you're just a dollar-a-day hired hand who's getting old and don't have a pot to piss in."

"You got me there, Sid . . . You sure as hell do. But what's that got to do with—?"

"This is *my* goddamn outfit!" he said poking a thumb into his chest. "And *my* horses and *my*—"

"All right!" I said tossing the dipper back into the bucket and walking off. "I don't give a shit— I'll catch any goddamn horse you want me to."

I caught the little bay, rammed a pair of bits into his mouth, led him to the barn, slung Sid's saddle on him, jerked the cinches into his belly, and was about to lead him right out to Sid—but he wouldn't untrack. "You little counterfeit!" I mumbled. Of course it wasn't his fault he wouldn't untrack. He was fat and fresh, and the way I'd bailed the cinches into him it was a wonder he didn't pitch over on top of me or fall over backward. Instead, he did me a favor and just swelled up like a toad.

I calmed down some and loosened his cinches. Then I led him out of sight of the door and got on him and trotted him around inside the barn for about a minute to get the kinks out of him. I still didn't care what he did to Sid, but I didn't want to have to face Judith if something happened and I hadn't done what I knew I should've done.

When I got off and led him outside, Sid was standing by the corral.

I led the horse next to Sid, tossed the right rein over the horse's neck, and handed the left to Sid.

"Whoa, Banjo," Sid said as he let go of the fence with his left hand and put it on the saddle horn. When I made a move toward him, Sid stopped me with a look. "If I need help from you, I'll tell you." He stood there a few seconds on unsure knees with arms outstretched, his right hand still on the fence, his left on the saddle horn. Then he released the board and grabbed the saddle horn with the right hand as well.

"Put my foot in the stirrup and push me up," he said. Once in the saddle, Sid struggled with his left foot, trying to move it enough to slide it into the oxbow. "I can't do it," he said.

I took his foot and put it in the stirrup. "Maybe you need some wide-bottomed stirrups."

"I'll use whatever goddamn kind of stirrups I want," Sid said.

I looked up at him. "I don't care if you use any stirrups at all. I don't even care if you fall off . . . just don't expect sympathy from me if you do. Hell, nobody ever has sympathy for me when I wind up lookin' at a horse's belly."

"And I bet you've done that often enough."

"I sure as hell have," I said, turning away from him to go get my own horse. "I saved the bags on the bull calves and the ears on the heifers—do you want me to count the cows out the gate or do you want to?"

"I'll count 'em," he said. Then he rode off.

Shorty looked at me like I'd done something terrible when he saw Sid on the bay. "Don't look at me," I said. "It's his horse and his outfit—he told me so."

We held the cattle up at a water hole in the shipping pasture only a quarter mile from the corrals and were riding back to the barn when a cottontail rabbit jumped out from a clump of beargrass just as Sid's bay put his right front hoof down three inches from it. The bay snorted and jumped two feet to his left, and Sid was left hanging at an awkward angle to the right—which boogered the bay worse than the rabbit had. The horse spun around twice to the left and slung Sid the length of the bridle reins out of the saddle and onto the ground.

"Damn!" he said as he pushed himself up into a sitting position.

"Are you hurt?" I asked as I stepped off my horse, thinking I should've ridden the bay a little longer or even better yet never have caught him in the first place.

"Yeah . . . ," Sid whispered, and wilted onto his back again into the grass. "And it's all your fault."

"Dammit!" I said, disgusted at the whole chain of events as I knelt in the grass beside him. "You shoulda listened to me, dammit! Now . . . ."

"I think the bastard crippled me," Sid moaned.

"You think what?"

"I said I think the bastard crippled me!"

Me and Shorty looked at each other, and then we both looked at Sid.

"Hell, you were already crippled!" I said.

"I was?" Sid sat up and ran his hands over his body. "Thank god!"

Shorty and I saw a slow smile begin to creep across Sid's dirty face.

"You son of a bitch," I said.

Sid started laughing, and then Shorty started laughing. In a few seconds the three of us were laughing—Shorty sitting on his horse, me kneeling in the grass, and Sid lying back and laughing into the sky.

CHAPTER 11

AFTER WE UNSADDLED and washed up in the trough in front of the barn, we gathered around the table to eat all we could hold of beans, beef, gravy, homemade bread, and okra while we talked and laughed about the day's branding. When we first mentioned Sid getting on a horse, Judith stopped eating and looked up. "Sid . . . *you* were on a horse?"

"Well . . . ," Shorty said, answering for Sid, "when he wasn't on his back at the ends of his bridle reins lookin' up at the sky, he was."

"Good god, Sid!" Judith said, then looked at me.

I raised my eyebrows. "Don't look at me!" I said.

"I'd think you'd be glad I was on a horse again," Sid said.

"Well . . . I am," she answered. "But you could have been killed!"

"And wouldn't you be the grieving widow?" he said.

The laughter suddenly went out of Judith's eyes. She looked at him for several seconds, but just when I thought she was going to respond, she pushed her chair back and stood up to get the plum cobbler off the windowsill.

"Glad you could help us, Shorty," Sid said as we passed the cobbler around the table.

"Don't thank me," Shorty said. "Thank your highly paid cow boss. I wanted to leave for Mexico the day I quit Shiner's."

Sid looked at me. "So you're planning on leaving now, too?"

I glanced at Judith. She looked at me and then looked down at her plate.

I swallowed some cobbler and said, "I figured you might want us to push the cattle back into the two big pastures and maybe prowl for worms for a few days. Or we can be gone in thirty minutes— it sure won't take us long to—"

"What about it, Judith?" Sid asked.

"What about what?" she snapped.

"What about Concho staying for a few more days, and Shorty too if he wants to?"

"That's up to you," she said flatly.

"But don't you think it's been better around here since Concho came?"

"Of course it has!" she said. "The horses are home, the cattle are home, the fences are up, the water gaps are in, the calves are . . ."

Sid looked at me with a smile that was hard to read. "I guess, since it's all right with Judith, maybe you ought to stay a few more days if you can."

"All right," I said, and put another bite of cobbler into my mouth without looking up.

"Get us some cigars," Sid said after we were through with dessert.

When Judith came back with the cigars we— me, Shorty, Juan, and Pablo—thanked her for the meal and went outside.

Sid paid Juan and Pablo for their three days' work and they left with their well-earned money and cigars. Then me and Sid and Shorty sat in the shade of the porch and lit our cigars.

Before we were finished with the cigars, Judith opened the screen door and said, "I think we all ought to go to town tonight."

Sid looked up at her. "What for?"

"They're having a dance at Grady Vinson's new barn before he puts lumber in it—he told me about it when I was buying groceries. I think getting the calves branded deserves a little celebration. I can bring some of the food we have left over and—"

"What would I do at a dance? For god's sake, Judith!"

But this time Judith wasn't in the mood to back down. "Not everyone dances when they go to one of those things, you know that. I just thought it would be fun to get off the ranch for a little while. It's still early—there's plenty of time to take a bath and rest before we'd need to go."

"Sounds good to me," Shorty said.

"Come on, Sid," Judith pleaded, "the only time you've been off the ranch in months was to go to Bob Shiner's funeral."

Sid seemed to think about it for a few seconds, and I thought I knew what his answer would be, but he surprised me. "Okay," he said, "we'll go. I'd love for Little Bob to see me there with the two best hands in the basin."

"Concho, you're welcome to come, too," Shorty said.

"Well, that's mighty nice of you, Shorty," I said.

"Just don't get in the way while Sid's showin' me and Judith off," he added.

"I'll try not to," I said as I stood up. "Now, I'm going up to Drippin' Springs and rinse off this dirt and blood and branding smoke. Are you coming—or are you going to stay here till Sid runs out of cigars?"

"I guess I'd better go with you," he said. "There may be some homely-lonely at the dance who might not notice my charm if I don't clean up a little."

We came back down an hour before sundown and hitched Hank to the buggy. Shorty decided he ought to go on a saddle horse in case that homely-lonely got him cornered and he couldn't get loose in time to go back to the ranch with us.

We'd both shaved our sun-red faces and bathed in the spring. I had on a pair of clean Levis and a clean white shirt with the top button buttoned. I'd even knocked all the dust I could off my hat and cleaned the blood and manure off my boots as best I could. Of course Shorty said it was a shame Judith wasn't there, because then I could've taken a bath and washed my clothes and boots all at the same time.

I pulled the buggy to the yard gate, and Sid came out of the house on his crutches, dressed much like me and Shorty except that his clothes were newer. He wore a shirt Judith had ironed and a string tie, and he didn't have to wear the same hat and boots he'd been branding in. He was also carrying a bottle of whiskey in his right hand.

About the time Sid got to the gate on his crutches, the screen door opened again and Judith stepped out onto the porch, wearing a yellow dress with a white ribbon in her hair and carrying a big basket of food with a blanket over the top of it. The dress didn't have any lace or ruffles on it, and I guess it would have been called a plain dress. On Judith though, with the yellow against her tan skin and her eyes full of life and her hair clean and brushed as soft as tickle grass, there was nothing—nothing in the world—plain about that dress.

As we drove down the wagon road toward town, the sun was low in the west and throwing its last soft rays against the north rim of the basin, turning it different shades of yellow and gold.

Here and there, where the rim jutted out, it cast long shadows on its recessed portions.

"Isn't that beautiful!" Judith said.

"It sure is," I said.

"It's called Devil's Rim," Sid said. "See the devil's face?"

"No," I said. "I don't see it."

"I never have either," Judith said.

"See that outcrop right there . . . right above the bend in the creek?"

"Yeah . . . but I don't see the devil's face," I said.

"It's right there!" Sid sounded irritated. "Those creosote bushes on the rim make his horns, his eyes are those rocks, his nose is that bush growing out of the wall and—"

I shook my head. "I still don't see it."

"I just see something beautiful," Judith said. "And I don't choose to look for something evil in something so pretty."

"Just because you refuse to see something doesn't mean it's not there, and—"

"I'm not refusing to see it!" Judith snapped. "I *don't* see it! Besides, what difference does it make if I see it or not? Good lord! Let's just drop it!"

But Sid wasn't ready to drop it yet. "The Apaches who were here before the white man came said their ancestors lived in peace and harmony until the devil came off the rim one day and lured them into sinning and God turned His back on them. Some—"

"The Apaches never heard of the devil or God, either one, until the white man taught them," I said.

Sid ignored me. "Some think the devil still lives up there in that rim and that every bad thing that happens here is because of him—like that horse falling on me right after we were married."

"My god, Sid!" Judith said. "Surely you don't believe that?"

"Did I say I believed it?" He paused. "But sometimes I wonder."

"I still think we see what we want to see," Judith said in a calmer voice.

Sid was quiet for a few seconds and then said, "Which direction did you come from to get to the basin, Concho? I never did hear you say."

I pointed to the rim. "I came right off that rim right there—off the trail next to that big outcrop."

Sid nodded. "That's called the Devil's Trail," he said.

"Then I followed the Devil's Trail off Devil's Rim," I said. "But that old devil must've been laid-up somewhere because I dang sure never seen him. And when I stopped at the creek and let the horses water I never seen a single devil there, either."

"Not even his reflection?" Sid asked with an antagonistic little laugh.

"The only reflection I saw was mine," I said. "And I've been dehorned."

"Will you both stop!" Judith said. "If we can't carry on a halfway intelligent conversation, let's just ride and enjoy the evening."

By the time the sun had been set long enough to let the evening star shine bright over the basin we'd got close enough to town to hear fiddle music.

"That sounds good, doesn't it?" Judith said. "Sounds happy. You know, I honestly believe that's the first music I've heard since the day we got married."

"That old boy's really sawin' on that fiddle," I said. "Makes it hard to keep your feet still."

Sid uncorked his bottle and took a swig from it.

Grady Vinson's barn was open sided, but three wide strands of ribbon had been tied between each stud and bales of hay had been laid in front of the ribbon for people to sit on.

People were dancing to the music inside, and others were carrying in food from their wagons. Other people, mostly men, were milling around on the sidewalk and in the street, leaning on wagons and talking and passing bottles of whiskey back and forth.

I got the buggy as close to the door as I could so Sid wouldn't have to go any farther than necessary on his crutches. Sid took a drink and held the bottle toward me.

"No thanks," I said, and shook my head.

"Still too good to drink with me?"

"No," I said, "but I've fought the bottle long enough to know it's bigger than I am."

"You're just too damn good to be true, aren't you. Just too much candy for a dime."

"I don't know, and I don't know which you're more of . . . drunk or crazy."

"If you're just dyin' to get rid of some of that stuff, Sid," Shorty said after he'd tied his horse to a buggy wheel, "I'll sure oblige you."

I got out of the wagon, and Sid handed the bottle to Shorty. "At least you're not too good to drink my whiskey, are you."

Shorty took a long pull on the bottle and lowered it. "No sir," he said with a smile.

"Shorty's not too good to drink anybody's whiskey," I said.

Shorty helped himself to another long pull, handed the bottle back to Sid, wiped his mouth with the back of his hand, and said, "Much obliged—if you need any more help with it, just holler." He turned toward the barn, made an odd movement with his shoulders, and walked away.

I helped Sid out of the wagon. "I don't need any more help," he said when he was on the ground. Then he looked at the barn and all the people in it and said, "Come on, Judith, I guess it's time to show the good people of Chugwater Basin how poor old crippled Sid and his mail-order bride are doing. This'll make the trip to town worthwhile by itself for some of 'em."

We walked into the barn; we were greeted by a soft flood of coal-oil light coming from three rows of lanterns hanging from strands of barbed wire tied to ceiling joists at each end of the building. Two fiddles, a bass fiddle, a dulcimer, and a guitar provided music for the caller: *"Join hands and circle to the left; circle right back and swing your pard; and the lady on the left, swing your mate; now hurry up gents and don't be late . . ."* Judith pointed toward two long tables set up along the wall, which had food on them. The three of us walked together across the new wooden floor, with Sid in the middle. I sat the basket on the end of the first table and watched Judith take the blanket off the top of it and spread the food out on the table.

"Ducks in the river, going to the ford; coffee in a little rag, sugar in a gourd . . ."

The dance floor was crowded, but it seemed like everyone who wasn't dancing or clapping their hands to the cadence of the caller's voice was looking at us, or at least had looked at us. Even some of those who were clapping glanced at us without stopping their hands, and some of these elbowed the person next to them who turned to look, too. Several people came by and shook hands with Sid and nodded to me and Judith.

"Well, if it's not the Vans," a man's voice said. I turned my head to see Malcolm Floyd all dressed up in a pair of tight-fitting, Ogden Miller plaid wool jeans, smiling and looking at Judith.

"Hello, Malcolm," Sid said.

"How you doin', Sid?" Floyd replied without taking his eyes off Judith. "You really look pretty tonight, Mrs. Van."

Judith said nothing.

Two women walking past us on their way to the food tables caught Malcolm's eye. "Hello, ladies," he said. "I sure hope there's a place for me on your dance card."

One of the women tilted her head and said, "Maybe," with a flirtatious smile as she and her friend stepped up to the food table.

Malcolm looked back at Judith. "I'm sure Sid won't mind"—he smiled slow and cocky—"and I'd be honored if you'd dance with me later." He left without waiting for a reply.

"That son of a bitch," Sid mumbled, which was the first thing Sid and I had agreed on in days. Up until that moment, even after he'd used a cedar stay on me, Malcolm had meant no more to me than a counterfeit horse in someone else's string that I was glad I didn't have to throw my saddle on—someone else's problem and not mine.

But all of a sudden he was more than that. It wasn't so much the fact that he'd acted like I wasn't even there as it was the disrespect he'd shown Judith. The look in his eye and the way he smiled was the look and the smile of a man who was thinking only one thing—that he knew what the woman he was talking to needed and that he was the one she needed it from.

"Let's just go home," Judith said, shaking her head slightly and closing her eyes for a moment.

"No, let's get some of this food and sit down on a bale of hay," I said.

She didn't say anything for a few seconds. Then she said, "Okay . . . what do you want to eat, Sid?"

"Nothing," he answered.

"Well, Concho and I are going to get a plate of food and sit down on this bale of hay right behind us."

"Okay," he said as his eyes swept across the faces in the barn.

"Are you going to sit down with us?" she asked.

"Yeah . . . in a minute."

Shorty came to the table and started filling a plate with food while Judith and I were filling ours. "Why, Shorty," I said, "I figured you'd have a dry hemmed up by now."

"What do you think about that one right there?" he said in a low voice, looking across the table and down it a little ways to a woman who was smiling at him. "She looks all right," I said. "I'd hate to be around her in a rain, though—she'd look real funny if all that paint was to run down to her feet."

"Yeah," he said, smiling back at the woman, "but in this lantern light that paint don't show up much and shows up even less in the moonlight."

"Well, you'd better head her before she gets with the bunch and goes to millin'."

When Judith and I had gotten our food we sat down next to each other on the bale to eat while Sid leaned on his crutches a dozen feet in front of us. "That man makes my skin crawl!" Judith said.

"What man?"

"Malcolm Floyd!" she answered. "Any time we happen to be in town at the same time and he sees me, he has to come talk to me and tell me how pretty I look. One time I'd been swimming at Dripping Springs and had just put my clothes back on when I saw him standing by the corner of the cabin. He said he'd just gotten there, that he was looking to see if there were any Shiner cattle there, but I know he watched me get out of the water and get dressed. He said we ought to go in the cabin and have some coffee, that he knew how it must be for me living with Sid. That was the last time I was there until the day I was looking for you. I was afraid to go back."

"That son of a—"

"It's okay, Concho . . . but that's why I don't like him—in case you were wondering."

I didn't say anything for a minute or so. I couldn't do anything but think about Malcolm leering at Judith as she was getting out of the water without her clothes on. How could he think there was any way she'd even give him the time of day?

We watched Sid head for the door and disappear outside. "Want me to go see about him?" I asked.

"No," she said, shaking her head in an unconcerned manner. "I'm sure he's just going out to the buggy to get another drink." She seemed more relaxed than she'd been since we got there, and suddenly her green eyes regained their luster.

I looked down at my plate. "This is the first dance—"

"God . . . here he comes already," Judith said ducking her head.

"Who?"

"Malcolm."

I didn't duck my head—I raised it and looked Malcolm square in the eye when he was fifteen feet away and walking toward us. He didn't even stop or slow down when I stood up and stared at him, but I'd made my mind up that as soon as he got within arm's reach he would stop all right.

"No, Concho!" Judith said standing up beside me. "Don't spoil the night—please . . . Come on, let's go dance." She grabbed my hand and started walking toward the dance floor.

I'd been thinking about the possibility of dancing with Judith ever since it was decided we were all going to the dance. So when it came to making a choice between dancing or hitting Malcolm—even as badly as I wanted to hit him— it was a decision I didn't have to study on.

"That's a heel-and-toe polka," Judith said when we got to the dance area. "Can you do it?"

"I don't know," I said. "I've done it, but it's been a long time."

"You'll remember it once we get started," she said as she moved to my right side and held her right hand up toward her right shoulder. "Here, give me your hand."

I passed my hand behind her neck and took her right hand in mine.

"Now the other one," she said as she held out her left hand.

When I took her left hand she looked up at me and laughed.

"What?" I asked.

"You're stiff as a board! Lay your right arm on my shoulder and relax. Now it's right heel out, across the body with the foot and right toe down—heel, toe, heel, toe . . . come on, do it with me . . . heel, toe, heel, toe . . . that's it . . . now slide . . . slide . . . slide . . . now the left . . . heel, toe, heel, toe, heel, toe . . . you've got it."

The best that could be said about the heel-and-toe polka was that somehow I stumbled through it. It had been fun trying though, and when the music stopped we were both laughing.

Then the fiddler started up again. "That's 'Old Rosin, The Beau,'" I said.

Judith looked surprised that I knew the name of the tune. "Do you waltz?" she asked.

The fact was, all afternoon when I was thinking about the possibility of dancing with her, it was a waltz we were doing, and I wasted not a second in taking her left hand in mine, putting my right hand on her waist, and finding the rhythm of the music.

"Well . . . I'm impressed!" she said as we waltzed across the floor.

"I know Malcolm's already beat me to it and told you how pretty you look," I said as I looked down at her. "But I'll go him one better and say you're the prettiest woman here. When you walked out of the house this afternoon . . ." I stopped and smiled and just shook my head.

We danced a quarter way around the floor before she raised her head and asked, "How come you've never gotten married . . . or have you?"

"Not even close."

"Why?"

I shrugged. "The most I've ever had in my life, Judith, is what I've got right now—two saddle horses and my blankets. Now, wouldn't I have had a lot of business gettin' married?"

"Shorty said you were a wagon boss on a big ranch in Arizona for three years."

"Yeah, I was."

"Can't wagon bosses get married? I think Otto Brooks is."

"I guess they can, but I never did."

"Why'd you leave that ranch?"

"The bank took it over . . . and I adiosed."

"Some woman should have gotten you, Concho, and settled you down."

"Lucky for womankind none of 'em did."

"You mean you've never been in love?"

"Any cowboy who's slept out with a roundup wagon for any length of time or spent two or three months going up the trail's been in love—madly in love—usually with the first woman he sees when he gets to town, and that lasts about—"

Suddenly I was embarrassed.

"About thirty minutes?"

"Yeah . . . countin' the bath and all."

"You're blushing, Concho," she said with a pretty smile.

"I know it. Now you see another reason I never got married."

"Why? Because you're modest and decent and—"

"I'm not all that decent," I said.

"You've always been decent with me."

"Yeah . . . ? Well, it's a good thing you can't read my mind."

"Why . . . Concho!" she said with a look of teasing shock as we made turn after turn across the floor, either looking into each other's eyes or Judith holding her head back and laughing while the hair fell away from her neck.

The waltz had been even more than I'd hoped for when I'd dared hope we'd get to dance together at all, Judith prettier, happier, and more at ease—but now, all too soon, it was coming to an end.

"There's not many things sweeter in a cowboy's life than waltzing to a good tune with a pretty woman in his arms," I said.

"I'm glad you're staying for a while," she said more softly as we were completing the last turn.

"I can't stay forever, though," I said as the music stopped.

"I know," she whispered as she looked into my eyes and gave my hand a squeeze before releasing it.

I glanced toward the bale of hay we'd been sitting on and where our plates of food were and saw Sid leaning on his crutches a few feet in front of it, watching us.

I walked to the bale, picked up my plate, and sat down without looking at him while Judith went to him and asked if he was ready to eat.

"No," he said, "but you and Concho'll probably need to fill your plates again—it looked like you were working up your appetites."

Judith sat down on the hay beside me, and we'd eaten only a few bites when she gestured with her head toward the door where Robert Shiner had just walked in with a woman beside him. "That's his wife—Flora Lee," she said. "I've met her only a couple of times, but she's always been nice to me. I guess we're going to find out if Robert and Sid will speak to each other, because they're coming over here to the food tables."

161

"Who's that couple with 'em?"

"That's Harry Stiles and his wife, Helen. Harry owns the bank, and he's the mayor too."

"Hello, Sid," Harry Stiles said.

"Hello, Harry," Sid said as they shook hands. "How are you, Mrs. Stiles?"

Sid and Robert Shiner looked at each other and nodded like two dogs circling each other with their tails up.

"Harry and I were just talking about you," Robert said.

"Is that right?"

"Yeah . . . maybe we can do each other a favor."

"I can't imagine how," Sid said.

Flora Lee Shiner and Mrs. Stiles spotted Judith sitting on the bale of hay and stepped around the men to speak to her.

Judith and I both stood up, and she introduced me to the women. They made woman-talk—about dresses and hair and gardens—while I drew little patterns in the dust on the floor with the toe of my boot and listened more to the men talk.

". . . and why would I do a fool thing like that?" I heard Sid say.

"Because I know how hard it must be to watch your ranch fall apart," Shiner said.

Sid fired back, "Hell! The fences are all up, the water gaps are all in, the calves are all branded, even the dries are separated. My place is in damn good shape!"

"But that's this year, Sid—and we both know why . . . because you were lucky enough to find a couple of drifters to help you. What about next year, though—and the year after that, and the year—"

"It's not for sale, period, Little Bob!" Sid's voice was getting louder.

"I'm willing to give you more than fair-market value for it. Because of where it is, it's worth more to me than it would be to anybody else. Don't give me an answer right now. Go home and talk it over with your wife—don't you think she—"

This time Sid's voice was so loud that it not only stopped the woman-talk but caused even the heads of nearby clappers to turn. "My ranch is none of my wife's business! Whatever decisions are to be made about *my* ranch will be made by *me!*"

I glanced at Judith and immediately saw not only the hurt and embarrassment in her eyes but the sympathy Flora Lee and Mrs. Stiles felt for her.

"Have it your way, Sid," Robert Shiner said. "Just remember, next time I may not be willing to be so generous."

The women smiled politely at Judith, then backed away and joined their husbands at the food table.

Judith and I sat back down on the hay, and I picked at my food.

Sid stood by himself for a few seconds and then went outside again.

I looked over at Judith and saw the tears brimming in her eyes.

"Do you want any more to eat?" I asked.

She was looking down at the plate in her lap and shook her head so slightly it was hard to tell it moved at all.

I was so mad at Sid I stood right up and went outside.

CHAPTER 12

SID WAS RIGHT where I thought he would be—leaning against the buggy with the bottle in his hand. "Judith is in there with tears in her eyes, embarrassed to death!" I said.

"Well, I'm sure you'll have her smiling again before the night's over, Concho," he said with a sarcastic grin.

"Now, just what in the hell do you mean by that?"

"You know what I mean, goddammit! When I pay you, I'll wonder if I'm not paying a stud fee—but at least my wife's smiling."

I hadn't planned on hitting him, but I did. I hit him on the right side of his chin with a short left hook. His head snapped back and blood started trickling from the corner of his mouth, but the wagon kept him from falling down.

He put a hand to his mouth, drew it back, and looked at the blood on it.

"I'm sorry, Sid," I said. "But you had that comin' and you know you did."

Then he hit me—and pretty damn hard, too—right underneath the left eye. I staggered backward a couple of steps and touched the spot where his knuckles had landed. There wasn't any blood on my fingers, but the bone underneath my eye was already sore.

"And you had that comin', too, by god!" he said.

"I might have," I agreed, gaining back the two steps his blow had cost me. "But not for what you said. We've never . . . hell, Judith wouldn't ever do that!"

"But you would, huh?"

"What difference does it make if I would or not? She wouldn't!"

"So . . . you son of a bitch, you've tried, huh?" And he hit me again right on the same spot underneath the same left eye and knocked me right back into the same tracks I was standing in after he hit me the first time.

I felt blood running down my face this time and wiped it off with the back of my right hand. "No, I haven't tried . . . and don't hit me again!"

"Just step right back up here and I will," he said.

"If I step back up there, *I'm* gonna hit *you* again. Damn, Sid, you're the bitterest son of a bitch I know! So you had some bad luck . . . you've still got the prettiest little ranch in the world and a wife that—"

"That don't even sleep with me . . . I guess if you was me you'd be all smiles."

"Maybe not . . . but I'd think I'd try to look at what I had instead of what I didn't have. And I wouldn't sleep with you either if I was her, not the way you treat her."

"Oh, you know so much about women, huh? Which whorehouse did you get your knowledge from?"

"Damn, Sid," I said again, only this time almost laughing. "You want to hear something funny? You're the kind of man I like, or usually do. You don't have any quit in you, do you. You're just like a horse that's got his mind made up to pitch and no matter how much you ooze 'im around or warm 'im up he's still going to swaller his head and pitch till he gives plum out. Then just as soon as he gets his wind he'll do it again. That's you— only you've got your mind made up to be bitter, and there's not a goddamn thing's gonna keep you from it, is there. What if you spent all the time and energy you put into being bitter and sorry for yourself into trying to make those legs work and being the kind of husband—"

"I'll be damned . . . it's not enough for you to just take over my ranch, now you're trying to tell me how to run my life *and* my marriage. I just wish to hell you'd stay out of all of it."

"I haven't taken over anything, Sid, goddammit! Haven't tried to. Don't want to! If

166

you'll remember, I was just passin' through this place, mindin' my own damn business, when I was *asked* to stay and help for a few days. Your damn place was falling down around your ears and look at it now! I guess you wish it was like it was before I came?"

"The ranch is in better shape—I can't deny that."

"Well, lordy me! Look out, folks, the sky's liable to fall—Sid Van's finally about to say 'Thank you, Concho'!"

Sid laughed. "I'm not *about* to say thank you— I'm not even about to come *close*. I just said my ranch was in better shape . . . but I'm not so stupid that I don't know why it is."

"Yeah!" I said. "I do too! Because I—"

"Because you saw a pretty woman married to a crippled man and you thought if you hung around here long enough you just might get you some of that! You haven't done a damn thing for me—I just happen to be the lucky beneficiary of the lust you have for my wife. So don't play the high-and-mighty Mister Savior to me, you son of a bitch!"

Sid had me there just as surely as if I'd been an old renegade cow suddenly caught out on an open flat. I had no way out, no way to get back to the rimrock. What I'd done, I hadn't done for Sid— and I hadn't done it for Judith strictly out of the goodness of my heart, either. Regardless of how noble I might have pictured myself when I was looking for those horses or fencing or water-gapping or branding, the truth was there, right there between me and Sid, and just like that cow looking at the cowboy between her and the rimrock, I saw no way around it.

"I got you there, didn't I," Sid said with a satisfied air. "You want to be thanked? Well then, just step right back up here and I'll thank you again."

"No," I said. "I'm tired of you hittin' me, and I can see it won't do any good to hit you again. So, what's the use?" I turned around to go back inside. It was only then that I realized that at least a dozen men had been standing behind me, and the one standing closest was Malcolm Floyd, looking at me and grinning.

"Sid don't like you pokin' his old lady, huh?" he said.

I hit him between the eyes with a left jab and followed that up with a right cross to the chin that drove him back and to the ground.

If he'd just lain there, I'd have stepped over him like stepping over a cedar post and gone back inside. But I wasn't all that disappointed when I saw him getting up. I was still in the mood to hit somebody, and at least Malcolm was somebody I could hit and feel damn good about it afterward.

Then somebody hit me on the back of the head. That turned out to be another top hand from the Shiner outfit, Billy Wright. If he'd been flanking me up at Smokey Hill like he was flanking Malcolm up that night, those cows would never have gone behind me and got away.

Just about the time my eyes stopped spinning from getting hit from behind by Billy, Malcolm hit me again in front. There were quite a few "attaboys" coming from the men standing around watching, but since I'd seen some other Shiner hands in the crowd I had a feeling none of the "attaboys" were for the underdog, which all of a sudden had turned out to be Concho Smith—again.

Malcolm and Billy both went to massaging my head in no particular order, and I had a disheartening thought that it looked like there was going to be a recurrence of what had happened the last time the three of us had been together on the ground. And, just like the last time, I heard the solid thud of hardwood striking flesh and the rush of air out of lungs.

Only this time it wasn't my flesh feeling the hardwood or my air I heard rushing out—it was Billy Wright's.

The cavalry had arrived—and although it arrived on crutches it was marching on fighting orders nonetheless.

Sid hit Billy across the back with a crutch that drove him into me and me into Malcolm. Although it was neither of their intentions to do so, Billy was sliding down my back dragging me down with him while Malcolm was holding me up.

My head was still spinning like a top, but when I saw the artillery coming my way out of the corner of my eye, my instinct told me to grit my teeth and duck for cover.

Malcolm tried to duck, too—I'm sure he did—but with me digging for cover underneath his chin and pinning his arms at his side in an effort to hold myself up, he didn't have much chance to avoid a fast-moving horizontal crutch, and he took a blow on the left side of his head that buckled his knees and melted him like wax in my arms.

When Malcolm went down I went down on top of him; I started clawing and scrambling to get out of the way because I saw Sid poised over us with a raised crutch, and I still wasn't certain exactly whose head that last blow was aimed at.

By then Billy had got his air back, grabbed Sid's arm, and was drawing back a fist when Shorty rushed up and cold-cocked him. Then somebody else—a big Shiner hand I'd seen at Smokey Hill, who they called Grande—rushed out of the crowd and stuck one on Shorty. But Shorty was as stout and as hard to knock off his feet as a buffalo bull, and his skull was about as thick, too. He blinked his eyes and tiptoed around and hit Grande the same time Sid landed a blow in the big man's ribs with a crutch.

Two other men who'd been at the Shiner wagon but whose names I didn't know jumped on Shorty then and I jumped in to help him. About that time Malcolm started getting up again, but out of the corner of my eye I saw Sid hobble over and go to work on him again.

Me and Shorty were doing all right with the two Shiner hands we had and Sid was giving Malcolm the kind of therapy he needed and everything looked pretty good until Grande came around and got back on his feet. On top of that, a couple of other men decided to throw themselves into the fray, and it became immediately apparent which side they had decided to side with.

All at once I saw a crutch flying through the air and reached up and caught it as it was passing by. I decided it would be handy as hell to use to chop Grande down to size. However, as soon as he grabbed it out of my hands and broke it over his knee and told me what he was going to do with the splinters, I decided that decision had been worthy of a little more forethought than I'd given it.

They were still dancing inside—*"Allemande left and do-si-do, grab your pardner and don't be slow; cowboy in the saddle, horse on the run; goin' to the big dance an' gonna have fun"*—but I had a feeling our set was about over with. What had looked so promising just a few seconds earlier now looked like it could very well be the Battle of the Little Bighorn in Chugwater Basin. Shorty and I were back-to-back, now delivering only half as many punches as we were receiving from the men coming at us. Sid was still swinging the one crutch he had left, and there was some hope in that, but not much when you considered the fact that he was now sitting on his butt as he swung it.

I didn't know who Denver was, but when I heard someone yell, "Better get Denver before someone gets killed!" I was all for the idea.

CHAPTER 13

WHEN THE SUN came up the next morning Shorty was looking out the window of the Chugwater jail, Sid was lying on the bunk, and I was sitting on the floor and leaning against the wall, thinking about what had happened before the fight—about Judith and how pretty she'd been, how it felt to waltz with her, holding her hand in mine, having a hand on her waist and even feeling the curve of her hip through her dress, thinking about everything we'd talked about and remembering the way she'd squeezed my hand when I told her I couldn't stay forever.

"I can't help but wonder what happened to that woman last night," Shorty said. "She was Sugar."

"I'm sure she was," I said.

"I mean, that was her name—Sugar. Said she'd just been in town a few days and didn't know anybody yet—said she was really glad we met."

"Quit whinin'," I said, rubbing my neck. "Nobody asked you to help us. We were doing all right."

"I could see you were—you were on the ground and Sid was fixin' to be."

"Concho couldn't knock me down," Sid said, looking up at the ceiling from the single bunk. "I don't see how Billy Wright could have."

"You'd have gone down if you hadn't been leanin' on the buggy," I said.

"Like hell," Sid said. "I wouldn't have gone down at all if somebody hadn't rolled into my legs. As long as I was on my feet there wasn't anybody going to touch me—not unless they wanted to eat a crutch."

"I damn near ate a crutch myself!" I said. "If I hadn't ducked just in time, I would have. I wasn't sure which head you were tryin' to hit!"

"From my end of the crutch it looked like I couldn't lose," he said. "You or Floyd, one head looked as good as the other to me."

"You should've heard what Judith said about Floyd when we were sitting on that bale of hay."

"I heard her—I'm crippled, not deaf. So where's the difference?"

I stopped rubbing my neck and looked at him. I started to say something but stopped, figuring what was the use. When Sid got something in his mind he wasn't going to change it until he was ready. But it didn't make me feel any better to hear that he thought Malcolm Floyd and me were alike.

"Denver!" Sid yelled.

He—Denver Jackson, the sheriff—came to the door that led from his office to the four cells and stopped. "Ya'll look like you've been through the ringer," he said with a grin.

"How come I don't see any Shiner hands in here?" Sid asked. "Just because Little Bob's a county commissioner doesn't mean—"

"Don't start that bullshit with me, Sid," Jackson said. "Everyone I talked to said ya'll were the ones who started the whole ruckus."

"And who did you talk to besides Little Bob?"

"A bunch of people. What—did you and Concho get tired of hitting each other and decide to just light into whoever happened to be handy?"

"When are we gettin' out?" I asked.

Jackson shrugged and reached for the cell key hanging on the wall. "Right now, I guess. I don't have any charges against you, just couldn't have you spoiling Grady's dance."

"Where's my wife?" Sid asked when Jackson unlocked the cell door and swung it open.

Jackson pointed toward Shorty. "She said she was going to ride his horse home. Your horse and buggy are right outside."

The only conversation on the way back to the ranch was this:

Sid said, "It's time for you to leave."

And I said, "We'll throw the pairs out of the shippin' trap as soon as we get back."

"No," he said. "I don't want you helping me anymore."

"Where're we goin'?" Shorty asked when instead of riding down the wagon road from the barn, I got off to open the gate going into the shipping trap.

"We just as well should throw these pairs into the east pasture," I said.

"I thought Sid—"

"How the hell is he gonna do it?"

We didn't say anything as we trotted across the shipping trap, but when I got off to throw open the gate leading into the east pasture, I guess Shorty'd held it as long as he could. "If you wanted under her skirt, you shoulda just done it and been done with it," he said, "without gettin' all—"

"Dammit, Shorty!" I said, looking up at him. "You know Judith and do you think she's *anything* like that . . . that Quiverin' . . . whoever she was?"

"No, I sure don't," he said. "But you'd a been a hell of a lot better off if she had've been, that's for sure."

"What does that mean?" I asked as I got back on my horse.

"It means I never once wondered if I ought to take old Quiverin' Ham with me when I left. Me an' old Jimbo never hit each other, and I never hit

175

somebody else who wanted to do the same thing as me. Hell, Floyd worked you over with a goddamn cedar stay, and you acted like it didn't even happen, but as soon as you heard he was wantin' to do the same thing you were, you dough-popped the hell out of him!"

"You sound like Sid now," I said. "Well, there's a hell of a difference between me and Malcolm Floyd."

"Yeah, you're right . . . You handle a rope better than he does."

I wasn't in any mood to argue with him. "You go that way and I'll go this way," I said. "I'll bet these old cows will be a damn sight easier to throw out than they were to throw in. They oughta be ready to take their calves and get outa here."

"What're you gonna do?" Shorty asked. "Throw up a teepee around your bedroll and make a house for her?"

I turned my horse around and rode off.

In an hour and a half or so I was closing the gate between the shipping trap and the east pasture. "Now, let's gather the dries out of the horse pasture and kick 'em in here."

"You know, Concho, men like us—"

"Shorty, I'm tired of hearing about 'men like us,'" I said as I trotted toward the horse pasture.

After we put the dries into the shipping trap I said, "I'll trot on over there and open the gate between the east and west pastures. Them old things will scatter themselves."

"Well, I'll go with you," he said. "You're not much company, but you're all I got right now."

I looked at him and laughed a little bit. "Not much compared to Sugar, huh?"

"I've been thinkin' about ol' Sugar all day," he said. "I just might have to go back to town tonight."

"I thought you were the one in a big hurry to rattle your hocks to Mexico."

"I am—but it's gonna be close to sundown by the time we get back to the camp, and I've always found it was bad luck to leave a camp late in the day."

"Unless you're going to town, you mean?"

"Yeah," he said and laughed, "unless you're going to town. You want to go?"

"No . . . I haven't lost anything in Chugwater. Besides, you know what they say—two's company but three's a crowd."

"That never bothered old Quiverin' Ham Pam."

"So you think Sugar may be another Quiverin' Ham Pam?"

"If she's not, I'm sure gonna do my best to turn her into one," he said. "I just truly believe there's not enough Quiverin' Ham Pams in this world."

I looked at him and raised my eyebrows. "I'm leavin' at sunup," I said.

After we'd eaten a bite at Dripping Springs,

Shorty cleaned up and saddled a horse. "Don't wait up for me," he said before he left.

"Don't worry about that. I'm going to saddle old Drifter and drive Sid's horses back to the horse pasture. Then I'm gonna take a bath in the spring and go to bed."

"You're not gonna get in any more trouble are you?" he asked as he leaned over his saddle horn.

"You'd better worry about yourself," I said.

"You know that's one thing about men like—" He stopped and grinned at me. "Adios, Concho."

"Give my regards to Sugar," I told him as he trotted off the bench. "And to Malcolm Floyd too, if you see him." In a lot of ways I wished I could have been like Shorty. Give him a string of halfway decent horses, enough room to unroll his bed, a Sugar every now and then, and he didn't need much more.

The gate where I put the horses into the horse pasture was about four hundred yards from the house and on enough of a rise so I had a good view of it over the corrals. After I shut the gate I stood by it and looked at the house for several minutes, hoping to see Judith, or hoping she'd see me and walk out to the barn. But I didn't see her, and if she saw me she didn't come outside. By then the sun was gone and a quiet, but one of the most lonesome dusks I'd ever seen had settled on the basin.

I knew that the thing between me and Judith had

gotten out of hand, but it seemed like I shouldn't leave without at least saying good-bye. On the other hand though, it seemed like that was exactly what I *should* do. One Concho Smith was telling me one thing while another Concho was telling me something else. Sid had been right about nearly everything he'd said about my reasons for doing what I'd done, at least to begin with—it had all been an excuse to hang around and maybe, as much as it hurt to admit it, "get me some of that." There had been nothing honorable or good in my intentions, and maybe, at that point, there really was no difference between me and Malcolm. Maybe Malcolm had been even more honest than I'd been—at least he'd been up-front with his intentions. But somewhere, somehow, that had changed, and sitting in that jail house I could have told Sid there was now a big difference between me and Malcolm—he just wanted to take his pleasure with her if he could, while I—though I didn't know how or why I'd let it happen—was in love with her.

Maybe Shorty was right—if I wanted to get underneath Judith's skirt, I should have just done it and been done with it; told myself it wasn't my fault Sid was crippled and she was unhappy and not getting what she wanted, and after all, a man like myself had a right to take his pleasure where he found it. If I'd done that, like Malcolm, or maybe even Shorty, would have, life would have been a lot less complicated for me and I wouldn't have even noticed what a lonesome dusk it was that had settled over the basin.

Then my heart stopped. The screen door opened and Judith walked onto the porch and stopped at the edge of it. I couldn't tell if she'd seen me or had even looked in my direction, but in a few seconds she stepped off the porch and slowly walked past the barn, stopped at the big cottonwood for a little bit, then walked to the top of the narrow draw that ran between the house and a line of trees on the other side.

Right or wrong, I got up on Drifter and circled to the right until I was out of sight of the house and trotted down to the draw.

I pulled up when I was a hundred yards down from where Judith was standing. We looked at each other a few seconds, and then I walked Drifter on down the draw and stopped again when I was thirty feet away from her in the bottom of the draw.

She turned her head and glanced toward the house. I stepped off Drifter and watched as she slowly walked toward me down the slope. She was wearing a blue-and-white gingham dress with nothing in her hair. Doves were cooing in the cottonwood beside the barn, making a sound like the wind blowing across the mouth of an empty bottle.

It seemed like I watched her walk down the

slope of the draw for a long time. She finally stopped about ten feet away, and for what seemed like another long time we looked at each other.

Then all of a sudden she was in my arms and my hands were in her hair pressing her lips against mine.

"Judith!" Sid's voice floated through the warm evening air, searching us out it seemed, and then settled into the draw around us.

Judith pulled her face away. "Concho . . ." She stepped back out of my arms.

"Judith . . ." I had no idea what I was going to say.

"Judith!"

She closed her eyes tightly for a second and shook her head. "He's on a tear . . . I've got to go in."

"Will you be okay?"

"Yes . . . but sometimes I wish . . ."

"Judith!"

She turned around, gathered up the long gingham skirt, and took a few steps back up the slope, then stopped and turned toward me again. "Are you leaving now?"

"In the morning," I said.

She started to turn back up the draw but stopped. "Is Shorty—?"

"He went to town."

She looked at me a second or two and then walked up the slope and disappeared over the top of the draw without looking back.

CHAPTER 14

ALL TRACE OF evening was gone by the time I got back to Dripping Springs, and it was nighttime in the basin. The promise of a full moon was apparent in the faint orange glow coming from beyond the curving steep wall of Big Butte Mesa, but for the time being, the only light afforded the creeks and springs was that coming from ten thousand star-specks in a black dome that stretched from towering rock rim to towering rock rim.

It appeared the basin was at rest, but I knew better. It was only the short period of quiet where passions satisfied by toil and sweat are exchanged for those of another kind, not yet satisfied.

I unsaddled Drifter and put him in the pen with Feathers and Shorty's other horse.

I took a quick bath in the spring, put on clean clothes, and made a pot of coffee while the moon slowly came around the wall of the mesa.

Time passed, slowly. The moon cleared the mesa wall and rose above it—rose above the short horse squabble in the pen behind the cabin, put to final rest by a well-placed hoof; rose above the sounds of fur and feather and warm-night insects; rose above the frog croaking at the foot of the bench where the springwater pooled again; rose above the firefly in the grass in front of the cabin lighted by a single coal oil lantern, and above the man on the porch restlessly waiting for a woman he wasn't sure was coming.

By the time the moon was beyond Big Butte Mesa, having drifted westward in its arc until it was somewhere above Smokey Hill, the man had given up and was lying asleep on top of his bedroll with his clothes on.

"Concho . . ."

"Concho . . ."

I opened my eyes and looked at the ceiling by the moonlight coming through the windows and the open door. I'd been dreaming that Judith was calling my name. It still hadn't cooled down much and I was sweating. I sat up on the edge of the bed and took my shirt off, thinking I should have slept on the porch.

I was reaching for my sack of Bull Durham when I thought I heard water splashing and wondered if the horses had gotten out or if it was just a raccoon messing around.

I stepped off the porch in my bare feet and stepped around the corner of the cabin so I could see the pen. The horses were still there.

The moon was far enough in the west now so half of the pool was in the shadow of the mesa wall and half was in the moonlight. At first glance I saw nothing and started to turn around.

I heard splashing again and saw movement in the shadows.

And then I saw her.

"Judith . . . ?"

She said nothing as I walked toward her in my bare feet through the gravel and sand and stopped at the edge of the water.

She was standing in water that reached halfway between her neck and her breasts moving her hands slowly back and forth for balance. She smiled at me and flung her wet hair back with a quick twist of the head.

"Hi," she said. "The water's cold when you first get in, but then it feels good."

Her clothes were in a pile on the bank to her right.

"Shorty's not here, is he?" she asked. "I saw your s . . . saddle but I didn't see his."

"No, he's not here," I said. "Where's your horse?"

"Hobbled on the other side of the pen."

"I was hoping you'd come, but then I gave up."

"I had to wait until I was sure Sid was passed out for the night.

"I can't tell you how many times I've thought about you and me, what it could've been like if we'd taken that swim in here without our clothes."

"I've thought about it a lot, too," I said.

"When you said I wouldn't think you were

decent if I could read your mind, was that part of it?"

"Part of it."

"Well, I've thought about it, too. I just didn't think I'd ever get up the courage . . . Are you going to just stand there with your britches on? This is getting kind of embarrassing, you know! Maybe you want me to put mine on."

"No! . . . I don't want you to do that."

"Well . . . then . . ."

I unbuttoned my Levis, pulled them off, and walked into the cold water until it was up to my waist.

"I told you it was cold," Judith said, laughing.

I took a couple more steps into deeper water and then bent my knees until the water was up to my chin.

"I can't believe it!"

"What?"

"That I'm actually swimming naked with a man in the moonlight! That I'm doing something nobody would *ever* expect of me! I can just hear the tongues clicking back home now—if they only knew!"

When I first saw Judith in the water and realized she didn't have any clothes on, it was strange but . . . I didn't know . . . I just . . . didn't know. But once I had my clothes off and was in the water, I started thinking again about some of the things I'd been thinking about for the past couple of weeks

185

and decided no man in his right mind would pass up a chance like what was before me in the moonlight, and I started closing the ten feet of water that separated us, trying to put whatever else might have been in my mind out of the way.

I stopped when I was a couple of feet away, close enough so I should have been able to see the sparkle in her green eyes in the moonlight, but I saw no sparkle.

"This isn't fair," I said.

"What's not fair?"

"You've seen me, but I haven't really seen you. You've been underwater the whole time, and with the moonlight shining on the water, I haven't really seen any more than I saw the last time—when you had your clothes on."

She giggled and I closed the two remaining feet separating us as quickly as I could. I grabbed her around her small waist, heaved upward, and released my hands.

Her body quickly came up out of the water to her waist and just as quickly disappeared back into it, head and all.

She came up spitting and coughing and laughing.

She flung her hair back again and wiped the water from her face with wet hands—hands, I noticed, that had no wedding ring on them. "Are we even now?" she asked.

"Only from the waist up," I said moving in to

kiss her. From the first words I'd heard her say after I'd come out of the cabin, I knew this was a different Judith I was with, but now that I was in the water with her and my eyes had seen her bare breasts in the moonlight and my hands had been on her bare waist I didn't care which Judith it was. I only cared about one thing.

She put a hand between our faces. "Wait!" she said and moved the hand and looked at me. "We can kiss—but no touching. Okay?"

"If that's the game you want to play, we'll play it," I said, moving my lips toward hers, expecting a kiss that would begin like the one we'd had in the draw that afternoon but ending in even more—much, much more—and hopefully on the bank or on the bed in the cabin.

But it was a short kiss, and nothing like I was expecting. She pulled away and moved back a step.

"What's the matter?" I asked.

She closed her eyes a second. "Nothing."

I moved in again.

"Wait a minute, Concho!"

"How much have you had to drink?"

"You smelled it, huh?"

"Yeah. I could tell by the way you were talking, too."

"I didn't have much," she said and tried to laugh. "It was the bottle Sid had been drinking from and there wasn't much left. I had a couple of sips while I was deciding whether or not to come here, and a couple more while I was saddling my horse, and then I had about three on the way before the bottle was empty. I didn't even think I felt it till just a few minutes ago."

"That's the way it happens when you drink it fast," I said.

"But that wasn't much to drink, was it?"

"For Sid or Shorty—or me a few years ago—no. But for somebody who's not used to it, it's quite a bit."

"Whew . . . maybe you're right," she said putting her palm to her forehead.

"Are you okay?"

"I'm dizzy . . . whew . . . am I dizzy!"

I helped her out of the water, then slipped my Levis on, and went inside to get a blanket. When I got back, she was sitting on the bank with her head in her hands, shivering.

I put the blanket around her and left my arm around her back. "Are you okay?"

"I don't know."

"It's no good, is it." I said.

"What?"

"Trying to be somebody you're not."

"I don't know who I am anymore, Concho—who I'm supposed to be. Judith Van? Who's that? I think I'm going to be sick."

"Let's go in the cabin," I said.

As soon as she stood up, she threw up. I held the

blanket around her and rubbed her back until she was through. "Can you make it inside now?"

She shook her head and threw up again.

When she was finished that time, I picked her up in my arms and carried her inside, where I laid her on the bed and put a blanket over her.

"Oh . . . god, Concho," she moaned.

"Gonna be sick again?"

"I don't know. Where are we?"

"In the cabin. I haven't lit the lantern. Just be still."

"How can you be still in a spinning cabin?"

I chuckled. "It'll quit spinning."

"When?"

"After a while."

"I'm sorry," she said. "Are you disappointed?"

"It's okay."

"I think I love you. Do you know that?"

It was a while before I spoke. "No."

"How did that happen?"

"I don't know," I said. "But I think it's happened to me, too."

For a while I thought she'd gone to sleep, but then she said, "Oh, boy . . . we're in trouble, aren't we?"

"Yeah . . . ," I said, "we are."

Again, it was quite a while before she spoke. "I shouldn't be here. We can't do this. Sid . . ."

"Is a damn bitter fool who—"

"I know but . . ."

"Yeah"—I sighed—"I know."

She put the back of her wrist on her forehead and I heard her breathing deeply. "You better help me outside . . . now."

That time, she not only threw up all she had, she tried to throw up a lot she didn't have.

When she lay back on the bed, I washed her face with a wet rag and gave her a few sips of cool, fresh springwater. When she was asleep, I tucked the blanket underneath her chin and looked down at her.

Was I disappointed?

Yeah, part of me—one Concho Smith—was disappointed for sure.

But the other Concho—the one I wasn't as familiar with and was still trying to decide whether I should like for his tenderness or loathe for his weakness—let his fingertips touch the soft, still lips of the real Judith and felt only a sadness for something he knew could never be.

Judith opened her eyes and looked at the ceiling just as day was breaking across the basin, about the time I'd told Shorty I was going to be leaving for Mexico. Shorty wasn't back yet.

Judith sat up slowly. She didn't say anything, but she moaned something or other that I couldn't make heads nor tails of.

"The next time you're going to be scandalous, you better remember how you feel right now," I said.

She seemed to remember only then where she was and fell back onto the bed, holding the blanket to her chin.

"Coffee?" I asked.

She nodded, and as I was pouring her a cup I saw her lift the blanket and peek underneath it.

"My god . . . ," she said as she brought the blanket back to her chin. "Did I . . . ? Did we . . . ?"

"You don't remember?" I asked as I handed her the coffee and grinned at her.

"I don't think we did, but part of it's a little fuzzy right now."

"You want the truth? We didn't."

She let out a long sigh. "Thank god!" She took a sip of coffee and looked underneath the blanket again and shook her head. "You put me to bed, didn't you?"

"Yeah."

"My god, Concho . . . what you must think of me."

"We went over that last night," I said. "Maybe someday you'll remember it."

She took another sip of coffee, then suddenly said, "Sid! Oh no!" When she swung her feet over the side of the bed and started to stand up she stopped. "Where are my clothes? I've got to get home! Maybe Sid drank so much last night he's not up yet."

I handed her the gingham dress and underclothes. "I'll saddle your horse while you put 'em on."

I stepped out to the porch and stopped when I saw thick smoke curling high into the morning air not far to the east.

"Judith!" I yelled.

"Oh . . . no . . . ," she whispered when she came outside.

"Hurry up!" I said, leaping off the porch and running to the pen to saddle not only her horse but Drifter as well.

Judith was beside herself with panic as she ran from the cabin and grabbed her reins from me. "Let's not think the worst!" I said, trying to calm her down but not feeling at all calm myself. *That was not grass smoke!*

CHAPTER 15

JUDITH SCREAMED.

I couldn't believe what I was seeing.

When we were getting on the horses I'd told her not to think the worst, but as we topped the ridge above Two Buttes Creek the worst was only a half mile away and plainly visible.

The house was engulfed in flames.

It was all but invisible because of the flames. Flames coming out of the windows and the front door and curling upward. Flames reaching higher into the sky than the top of the windmill or the tops of the tallest cottonwood trees behind the house.

The heat was so intense it stopped us before we

even got to the horse pens in front of the barn. By then the picket fence was beginning to catch fire in places and the leaves of the closest trees behind the house were beginning to burn.

If you've never heard a woman scream for someone she thinks is in a burning house, someone she thinks is in there because of something she did or didn't do, you've never really heard the human soul cry out in despair.

The porch collapsed in front of our eyes as we were jumping off the horses.

As we ran toward the inferno with our arms in front of our faces as a shield from the heat, the roof began giving way. But even with shields of arms, the fire was too hot. No shield of flesh and blood could withstand such heat without being cooked itself.

"NO!" I screamed at Judith.

When I saw she wasn't going to stop, I tackled her and lay on top of her while she cried and kicked.

I watched more of the roof give way. First a little more here and a little more there and then what was left in a loud *"swooshmm!"* that rolled the flames outward from the house and toward us.

The ball of fire was coming at us so fast I only had time to cover Judith as best I could with my body, put my arms over my head, and shut my eyes. It was the worst heat I'd ever felt, and I knew the singed hair I smelled was my own.

By the time it seemed safe enough to open my eyes and peek over my arm, what I saw made me shake my head in the most dumbfounded disbelief I'd ever experienced.

There was even more smoke, but there was less fire, much less. But then, there wasn't much house left to feed a fire, other than a portion of the north wall of the kitchen from where the sink had been to where it cornered with the east wall. That small part seemed content to smolder and smoke and shoot a few flames out from beneath the charred windowsill. The cookstove and icebox were there, but the oak table where only two days ago we'd all sat around and talked about the branding while we ate was black and smoldering and the legs holding up one end had either burned off or broken off when the roof fell. Part of the hall wall and about half of the back wall were left, too. Furniture held up portions of the charred roof and kept it from falling all the way onto the parlor floor. Same way with the bathtub and commode in the bathroom. Two metal headboards in different bedrooms were sticking through the roof, and the fireplace was blackened but as intact as ever, only now without the rest of the house around it, it looked naked and almost vulgar.

It was amazing, and frightening, that the house was gone so quickly, that it had all happened so quickly. No more than twenty minutes ago Judith and I were in the cabin, thinking our biggest problem was her getting home before Sid woke up.

I felt her sobbing underneath me, but when I got off her she wouldn't raise her head to look, as if by not looking the house would still be the same as when she'd left it in the moonlight.

"Sid could be in the barn or anywhere," I said. "I'll *bet* he wasn't in the house, or if he was, he got out. He wouldn't just sit there and let the house burn down around him. I know he wouldn't!"

That brought some hope back to Judith and she let me help her to her feet. "Let's find him," she said, wiping her nose and the tears off her cheeks with the back of a hand and only then daring to look at the burning rubble where the house had been. "Oh . . . *please,* Concho . . . let's find him!"

We ran to the barn as Judith yelled his name over and over.

When we didn't see him just inside the barn or find him in the tack room, I was afraid that as bad as it had been, we hadn't faced the worst yet. But Judith insisted on searching every stall and behind the barn, then the milking shed, the springhouse, the washhouse, and the well house.

She finally stopped her frantic, useless search and looked at me with a quivering lip and tears streaming down her smudged, dirty face. "Where is he?"

I looked at her but didn't say anything.

Judith got sick again, maybe partly from the alcohol the night before, actually only a few hours before, and maybe partly from the heat, but most likely from the grim reality she faced. I helped her to the shade of the cottonwood east of the barn and got her a drink from the pump.

Not a word passed between us for a half hour. The horses were grazing in the draw east of us, and I caught them and put them in the barn. When I came out of the barn, Judith was walking slowly toward the smoldering rubble.

"Judith . . . don't," I said.

She didn't stop.

The smoldering, charred remains of the house were now cool enough so you could stand within five or six feet and tolerate the heat. In a few places you could stand even closer than that. The leaves on the cottonwood trees behind the house had quit burning, but they were still smoking. The picket fence wasn't burning anymore, but the places where it had been burning were still smoking, too.

Judith was standing over where the kitchen had been when I saw the feet and calves sticking out from underneath part of the roof where the parlor had been. At first I thought it was just a pair of boots that the fire had burned the welt stitching on and caused the soles to curl. But then I realized those burned boots were at the end of a pair of charred legs.

"What is it?" Judith asked as she walked over to where I was.

I should have stopped her. When she saw what I'd been looking at, she got sick all over again and finally sat down in the scorched grass of the yard.

I tried to talk her into going back to the shade of the cottonwood east of the barn, but I got no response from her. She wouldn't look at me and she wasn't looking at the house. She just stared blankly toward the south.

I started to pick her up and carry her back to the shade when I heard a wagon coming. It was the fire wagon from town with three men on it. Sheriff Jackson and Shorty were horseback in front of it, and several other men were horseback behind it. They were all coming in a run, but when they saw Judith sitting in the grass and me standing beside her and the house already gone they stopped, and for several seconds all of them just looked.

Shorty and Sheriff Jackson walked their horses forward and stopped across the picket fence from us.

"We saw the smoke from town," Jackson said in a hushed tone. "What happened?"

Judith turned her head and looked up.

"Where's Sid?" Jackson asked.

When Judith still only looked at him, Jackson looked at me. I glanced at Shorty, then turned my head and nodded toward the boots and legs in the rubble.

Jackson and Shorty stood up in their stirrups for a better look. "Good god," Jackson said.

I looked at Shorty again and shook my head.

"Luther!" Jackson yelled.

A young man trotted up beside him. "Yes, sir?"

"Go back to town and get a wagon," Jackson said.

"What for?" Luther asked.

"What do you think for?" Jackson snapped.

"Well, I don't . . ." And then Luther saw. "Holy—"

"Get a stretcher from Doc Hammons, and a couple of blankets too."

"Yes, sir!" Luther said as he jerked his horse around.

"And Luther!"

Luther stopped his horse and looked back. "Yes, sir?"

"Tell Hammons there ain't nothin' he can do out here, but I want him to look at Sid's body when we get him to town. Well, go on—get out of here."

Jackson and Shorty got off their horses and walked through the yard gate so they could get a better look.

Jackson waved his hand to the other men, then looked at me. "What happened?" he asked again.

"I don't know," I said.

Jackson knelt down in front of Judith. "What happened, Mrs. Van?"

"There was a fire," she answered, almost in a whisper.

"How'd it start?"

"I don't know," she said.

"Were you asleep?"

She didn't answer.

"Sid's in there," Jackson said when the fire wagon pulled alongside the fence. "We'll have to wet down the area right there and cool it off enough to get him out."

The men started getting off the wagon, and the mounted men started getting off and tying or hobbling their horses. None of them said anything.

Jackson looked at me. "Were you here?" he asked.

"No," I said. "I was up at Drippin' Springs."

Jackson nodded and bent over Judith, gently taking her arm. "Mrs. Van," he said, "you might want to step over there by the barn."

"No—I . . . ," she started.

"He's right, Judith," I said. Then I looked at Shorty and said, "Shorty, why don't you take her over there under the tree and get her a drink?"

Judith stood up and looked at me. Then she went with Shorty.

The men formed a bucket brigade and began throwing water on the roof section over Sid, water that at first sizzled and popped and sent more smoke into the air but after a while only steamed.

"Wet it down all around there so we can walk on it," Jackson said.

199

I turned and looked to see how Judith was doing. She was standing beside Shorty underneath the tree, watching us. I knew she was blaming herself for not being there, blaming us for being together. Sid had put her through hell while he was alive and now he was putting her through an even worse hell, a hell that I knew would always be between us. So Sid was drunk and knocked over a lantern. Whose fault was that? Then I wondered—did he know she wasn't at home? If he did, then he knew where she was and no doubt was sure we were doing what we didn't do.

"Okay," Jackson said. "That's probably enough. Let's get our gloves and give it a try . . . Smith, is there a blanket around here anywhere?"

"Yeah," I said. "In the tack room. I'll go get it."

I got the blanket and then went into the stall where Drifter was and untied my gloves from behind the Cheyenne roll of my saddle.

When I got back, I dropped the blanket in the grass and took my place around the piece of roof over Sid.

"All right," Jackson said, "let's all lift at once and carry it that way." He gestured toward what would have been the north side of the house. "Ready? Now!"

The section of roof moved easily enough, but Sid's body was not so easily looked upon. I thought maybe the roof had protected the rest of his body from the fire, but it must have fallen on him too late for that. The rest of his body was in no better shape than his feet and his calves. One quick look was enough for me. It was hard to believe it was Sid. Even crippled and drinking too much, Sid had always seemed an overpowering presence wherever he was. Now he had been reduced to a silent charred corpse that barely looked human. The clothes were completely burned off him. So was his hair and most of the flesh on his face—eyelids, nose, lips, ears.

I turned and looked toward the tree to make sure Judith was still there.

"Let's get it over with," Jackson said. "Put the blanket right here next to him so we can roll him on it."

A man on each corner of the blanket picked it— and Sid—up. "Carry 'im out the gate and lay 'im over there by the fire wagon," Jackson said. "And fold that blanket over him."

Judith left the shade of the cottonwood and started walking forward. I met her midway and put my hands on her shoulders. "You don't want to see him, Judith," I said. "Please."

Jackson started toward us but was stopped by one of the men who'd arrived on the fire wagon. "Denver," he said "we're going to go ahead and throw all the water we have on the fire—or what's left of it. We'll throw some dirt around the edges, too."

Jackson nodded to the man and then walked on over to me and Judith. He pushed his hat back and took a deep breath. "Sorry, Mrs. Van. You don't have any idea how it started?"

"No," Judith said softly.

"I'm sure it started before daylight—did you say you were asleep?"

She didn't answer.

"Mrs. Van . . . ?" Jackson said. "Were you asleep?"

Judith was staring at the men throwing buckets of water on the smoking remains of the house. Finally she nodded her head.

"And you woke up and the house was already on fire?"

Again, after a while, Judith nodded.

"Sid must've already been up, already had his boots on. Had he been drinking?"

Judith nodded.

"Was he drunk?"

She shrugged. "He was last night."

"Might've knocked a lantern over," Jackson said. "But you didn't hear anything, huh?"

Judith shook her head.

"There'll be a wagon out before long to pick him up," Jackson said. "We'll take the body by Doc Hammons so he can look at it, and then we'll take it to the funeral home. Is that okay?"

Judith nodded.

"I'm sorry, Mrs. Van," Jackson said again. "I've known Sid a long time, and he was a good friend of mine, even though I hardly ever saw him after he got hurt. You're just lucky you got out alive." He started to walk away, but turned toward us again. "I was wonderin'—I guess you slept in that dress?"

"What?" Judith asked.

"You said you woke up and the house was already on fire—probably so much smoke you didn't have time to do anything but find your way to the door and get out—but you're wearin' a dress instead of a gown. So, I guess you must've slept in what you're wearin' now, huh? Or maybe you had some clothes in the washhouse, or some hanging on the line that you forgot to bring in last night?"

"What difference does that make now?" I asked.

"You're right—what difference does it make now," he said, stepping past us and walking toward the barn.

"Where are you goin'?" I asked.

"To see if I can find a couple more shovels," he said over his shoulder.

"Wait!" I said, thinking about the *two* saddled horses in there and how hard that would be to explain. "I know where they are . . . I'll get 'em for you."

He stopped and looked at me a moment, then said. "All right—get whatever you can find."

As soon as I got in the barn I went to the stall where Judith's horse was and jerked her saddle off him.

As I was standing in front of a saddle rack in the

tack room with Judith's saddle, Shorty stepped in the doorway. I looked at him and then slid the saddle on the rack. "No need to make things worse," I said.

"For who?"

"For Judith."

"She was with you, huh?" he said.

"Yeah," I said.

"What happened?"

"Nothin'."

"I doubt if Sid would say that," Shorty said.

"Probably not," I agreed.

"What about the fire?"

"I don't know—we hadn't been here long when ya'll got here."

"Damn."

"Yeah."

"Maybe you oughta tell Jackson the truth. You know—let the chips fall where they will."

"What good would that do?"

"I don't know—it's just kinda the way we've always done."

"This is different, Shorty . . . You ought to know that I don't give a damn if all the chips in the world fall on me—I just don't want 'em fallin' on Judith. If there was one good thing—just *one*— that could come from it, it would be different, but there isn't. It wouldn't bring Sid back. It would only make Judith look like . . . like something she's not. Hell . . . I've gotta find some shovels."

"There's a couple in the last stall," Shorty said. "You get them and I'll get the one out of the milkin' shed."

When we walked out of the barn with shovels the men were all busy around the fire. Judith was standing alone underneath the tree, staring at the blanket beside the fire wagon and the lifeless form wrapped up in it. "Here," I said, handing the shovels I was carrying to Shorty, "I'm going to see how she is."

"Are you okay?" I asked after I'd stood beside her for a few seconds.

"I wonder if he got out and then went back in to get me," she said without taking her eyes off the blanket. "Or if he was wondering why I didn't come help him."

"The smoke probably got him before he knew anything," I said, trying to make the unbearable a little less so. "He might've been asleep and never woke up."

"But he wasn't on the bed or the couch and he had his boots on—that's what I can't understand." She shook her head a few times. "I should've been here, Concho . . . If I'd been where I should've been, Sid would probably be alive. I'm so ashamed I even lied to Sheriff Jackson."

"Him knowin' where you were wouldn't change anything, Judith. And if you'd been here, Sid would probably still be dead and most likely you would be, too."

"But he was my *husband,* and I was with—"

"Don't do this to yourself, Judith—Sid could've been your husband but he chose not to be! He died just like he lived since the accident, drunk and bitter. There wasn't anything you could do about him living that way, and there's nothing you can do because he died that way. It's something that happened, Judith, and it's *not* your fault—not our fault!"

"But—"

"You think this is our punishment?"

"I think this is the worst possible thing that could have happened. Can you think of anything worse?"

"Yeah," I said. "If you hadn't come to Drippin' Springs, then you'd probably be dead, too—that would have been worse in my opinion. *This* was an accident, Judith. Pure and simple. But if you've got to blame somebody, then blame me. I knew what was starting to happen between us—I knew you were married and I knew I should have left. I knew all of that, Judith, but it didn't matter."

"But you didn't take the vows, Concho, and then break them. I'm the one who did that."

"And which vow did you break?"

"Concho!" She cut her eyes toward me. "I went to Dripping Springs with every intention of committing adultery."

"But you didn't!"

"And what if I hadn't gotten sick?"

"I don't think you could've done it anyway," I said.

"You just don't know, Concho . . . I *wanted* to do it. I could've done it!"

Sheriff Jackson walked over to us again, carrying a metal box about the size of a shoebox in his gloved hands, and stopped in front of us. "That's about all we can do right now, Mrs. Van," he said. "That wagon from town should be here pretty soon to take Sid in. What do you want to do?"

"I don't know," she said. "I can't think right now."

"Oh!" he said lifting the box. "We found this— it's got quite a bit of money in it, about a thousand dollars." He held the box in front of him and opened the lid. "Go ahead and take it out—the box is still pretty warm."

Judith pulled the money out, most of it in hundred-dollar bills. "There's some rings in there, too," Jackson said.

Judith put her hand back in the box and pulled out three rings—a wide gold band and a wedding set I recognized as Judith's.

"Yours and Sid's wedding rings?" Jackson asked.

"Yes," she said. "Sid hasn't worn his in months. I don't think he could ever get used to wearing a ring."

"I know," Jackson said. "I wore mine about two

months before I took it off for good. I didn't think most women ever took theirs off, though." You could tell it was a question.

"I don't usually take mine off," Judith said. "Just sometimes at night."

Jackson nodded. "Probably when you're gettin' ready for bed?"

"Yes," she said, looking at the rings in the palm of her hand before closing her fingers over them.

"Nice set of rings," he said. "I know this is hard for you, Mrs. Van. I hope that wagon . . . There it is now."

A buckboard pulled to a stop in front of us with the young man Jackson had sent to get it sitting in the seat beside another man. Behind the buckboard was a buggy with a fringed top, and sitting on the buggy seat were the two women who'd come over and talked to Judith at the dance—Flora Lee Shiner and Helen Stiles.

"Over there," Jackson said, pointing toward Sid's body.

While the men were loading Sid's body, Flora Lee and Helen stepped down from the buggy. "Oh, you poor thing," Flora Lee said as she hugged Judith. "I'm so sorry." Then she stepped back so Helen could give her a hug.

"What a tragedy for you!" Helen said. "We want you to come to town with us. The men can take care of things out here."

"I don't know," Judith said.

"Nonsense," Flora Lee said. "You need a hot bath, clean clothes, a bite to eat, and a soft bed. Come on, now."

"Go on . . . Mrs. Van," I said. "Me an' Shorty will take care of things out here."

"All right," Judith said. "As soon as they load Sid."

Sid was loaded quickly, and just as quickly Judith was on the buggy seat between Helen and Flora Lee, following the buckboard on the road to town.

Before he left, Sheriff Jackson stopped his horse in front of me and Shorty. "Are you two gonna stay out here and take care of Sid's things until Mrs. Van can get things straightened out?"

"Yeah," I said.

"It's a shame, ain't it?" Jackson said.

"It's worse than that," I said.

CHAPTER 16

AS SOON AS everyone was gone, I led Judith's horse out of the barn and turned him loose in the horse pasture. Then me and Shorty stayed around the burned house until we were sure that if the wind got up it wouldn't blow a spark into the grass and start a grass fire. Not long before sundown we trotted back up to Dripping Springs.

"So what are you gonna do?" Shorty asked while we were unsaddling the horses.

"Well, I can't hardly leave right now," I said.

"That's what I figured."

"Then let's go in the house and build a pot of coffee and fix us a bait of beans."

After we ate, I went out and cleaned up in the spring. When I went back inside, Shorty was stretched out on his bedroll. I blew out the lantern and lay down.

"So what are we gonna do tomorrow, boss man?"

"I thought you were asleep . . . I don't know. I guess we oughta see how many of them old cows went on into the west pasture and even 'em up a little before we close the gate. Then I better go to town and see when the funeral is."

"Are you fixin' to go to sleep?"

"Oh, sure," I said. "I bet I'll sleep like a baby after all that's happened today."

"Can you believe Sid letting that house burn down around him like that?"

"This morning when we first saw the smoke—God, it seems like that was ten years ago now—I told Judith not to think the worst. I doubt anything she could've imagined would've been worse than what we found."

There was no sleep at all for me that night. None.

In spite of what I'd said to Judith about the fire being nothing but a pure and simple accident, I couldn't help but feel my own guilt bearing down on me in the darkness.

I wished I'd never seen Chugwater Basin from

the top of Devil's Rim at the end of a long, hot day, never came off the Devil's Trail, never stopped that afternoon at the Van Ranch when a storm was brewing over Big Butte Mesa and Judith was trying to hang a gate in the wind.

And worst of all, I knew that whatever I was feeling, Judith was feeling it ten times—a hundred times—more strongly. We had known we were playing with fire, and we got burned. The funny thing was, both of us had been afraid of the fire from the beginning, and yet we were drawn to it like a couple of moths.

The next morning me and Shorty pushed another seventy-five pairs into the west pasture and closed the gate behind them.

As we were trotting back to Dripping Springs we saw five riders loping toward us across a wide sagebrush flat.

"Who in the hell do you reckon that is?" Shorty asked.

"Damn if I know," I said. "But if I was guessin', I'd say it's not just somebody from town out limberin' up their horses."

When they got closer we saw they all had rifles, either held across their bodies with both hands or the butts resting on their thighs and held with one hand.

"Looks like they're huntin'," Shorty said as they slowed down to a trot and began to spread out the closer to us they got.

"Yeah," I agreed. "But what?"

Sheriff Denver Jackson was in the center of the bunch, and by the time he was close enough for us to see the lines on his face the rest of the men had formed a half circle around us.

I looked at Jackson and then looked to the left and to the right at the rest of the men. Malcolm Floyd was in the bunch. Two of the others had been at the fire, and the other one I'd seen at the dance.

"Leave your hands right there on your saddle horn," Jackson said, his rifle laying across the saddle seat. "You too, Shorty."

"What's goin' on?" I asked.

"I'm takin' you in," Jackson said, looking straight into me.

"Takin' me in?" I said. "What for?"

"Sid didn't die in the fire."

"He didn't?"

"No," Jackson said, "he was shot first."

"Shot?"

"Tie his hands to the saddle horn," Jackson said without taking his eyes off me.

Malcolm got off with a piggin' string in his hand and handed his rifle to the man next to him. "What about Shorty?" he asked.

"No," Jackson said. "Just Concho—I've got a lady in town who swears Shorty was with her all night."

"Just a damn minute!" I said, holding a hand up when Malcolm started toward me.

"Men!" Jackson said.

Three rifles came up cocked, pointed at me.

"Go ahead," Malcolm said with a smile as he stood by my right stirrup, pulling his piggin' string through his hand. "Do something stupid like you usually do."

"You don't think I shot him!" I said, looking back at Jackson.

"Put your hands back on the saddle horn," Jackson said.

"Well, hell . . . wait a minute! Let's talk about it."

"We can talk in town," Jackson said.

"I've never been one to tell you what to do," Shorty said as he twisted in his saddle and looked at the rifles pointed at us. "But if I was you, I think I'd put my hands on the saddle horn like he says."

I looked at Jackson a few seconds. "Okay," I said. "I'll go in with you, but there's no need to tie my hands."

"You're not the one callin' the shots," Malcolm said.

"And you're not either, Malcolm," Jackson said without taking his eyes off me.

"This son of a bitch here's not tyin' *anything* on me," I said.

"All right," Jackson agreed, nodding his head. "I'll tie 'em then." And he stepped off his horse with his rifle.

"Have you talked to Judith?" I asked as he and Malcolm met in front of my horse and exchanged piggin' string and rifle.

"Should I?" he asked.

I didn't say anything.

"Concho . . . you've got to do this my way," Jackson said as he stepped to my horse's left shoulder, holding the piggin' string. "Hand me your reins and put your wrists on each side of the horn. When we get back to town maybe we can sort this all out."

"But why do you have to tie my damn hands?"

Jackson let out a long breath. "It's just the way it's gotta be done."

I shook my head in disbelief. I wanted to fight and I wanted to run and I wanted to shake some sense into somebody's head. "Why would you think I'd do anything to Sid?" I asked.

Jackson looked at me and didn't say anything.

"Hell, if he wants to run, let 'im," Malcolm said as he pulled back the hammer on Jackson's rifle. "Be quicker and easier."

"Malcolm, goddammit!" Jackson said. "I told you that if you came, you'd have to keep your mouth shut! Now, uncock that rifle!"

"After you get him tied," Malcolm said. "Feller sorry enough to do what he's done . . . Hell, there ain't no tellin' what else he might do."

Jackson stepped around my horse's head and stood in front of Malcolm. "Give me my rifle," he said.

Malcolm looked at me and grinned, then uncocked the rifle and handed it to Jackson.

Jackson tossed the rifle to another rider and then stepped up to my horse and looked up at me again. "Don't make this any harder on any of us, Concho. If you're innocent, then you don't have anything to worry about. We'll go to town, and I'll listen to what you have to say, but I've got to tie you up—for everybody's safety."

"Damn!" I said thinking about having my hands tied to the horn where I'd be helpless. "Damn! Damn!"

I let out a long breath, shook my head, and finally put my hands on the saddle horn.

Feeling that piggin' string draw my wrists so tight against the saddle horn I could barely move my fingers, and then having it wrapped three times behind them and finally double-half-hitched back over the top of the horn was the worst feeling I'd known.

Malcolm looked up at me and sang lowly and slowly and with a grin I'd have liked to've shoved down his throat, *"Come along boys . . . tell you a tale . . . of Concho Smith on the devil's trail."*

CHAPTER 17

IF ANYONE IN town didn't already know that Sheriff Jackson had deputized some men and gone after me, the word spread from one end of town to the other like wildfire as soon as the first person saw us hit the west end of Main Street.

215

People came out of every business and stood on the boardwalk and watched as we passed by. Grady Vinson and another man stepped out of the mercantile and watched us. A man getting a shave in the barbershop even stepped out to watch with lather on his face and the barber's bib around his neck. Three women came out of the dry-goods store and stared and whispered to each other as we passed by. A boy ran along the boardwalk in front of us, sticking his head into every door. Before he'd even get to the next door, heads were sticking out of the door he just left, followed by people stepping out.

Malcolm sang in the same low tone behind me: *"Concho Smith coming to town . . . with his dander up and his hands tied down."*

As soon as we stopped in front of the jail, Sheriff Jackson wrapped my reins around his saddle horn and stepped off. He walked back to Malcolm and said, "Malcolm, you'll never wear a deputy's badge for me again. Now, let me have it." Then he said to the other men, "If ya'll will help me get him inside, you can go . . . and thanks."

Jackson untied my hands from around the saddle horn and stepped back while the other three held their rifles pointed toward the ground and watched.

A little past high noon I heard the heavy clank of the steel door slamming shut in the hot, stuffy cell. By then I'd been in the basin a little less than one month.

"You're gettin' to be one of my steadiest customers," Jackson said from the other side of the bars. "Now, we can talk. What do you have to say?"

"What do I have to say? . . . You're crazy as hell—that's what I have to say."

"And that's it?"

"Why do you have *me* here? Because I'm a stranger and I happen to've been workin' for Sid? What about Malcolm or Robert Shiner? . . . Hell, Sid might've killed himself for spite—I've seen snakes mad enough to bite themselves, but I've yet to see one as mad as he was."

"And why was he mad?"

"Because he was crippled. He was bitter at the world—you know that."

"But you said he was mad . . . mad and bitter aren't the same things."

I didn't say anything.

"What reason would Malcolm or Robert have to kill him?"

"Malcolm made an indecent proposition to Judith, and Sid worked him over pretty good with that crutch at the dance," I said. "And Shiner wanted his ranch but Sid refused to sell it."

"Robert Shiner already owns a big part of the basin. Why would he kill a man just to get another little piece of it? Besides, I've known the Shiners for years and years—it's not their way to go around killing anybody, much less a crippled man."

"And you think it's *my* way?"

Jackson shrugged. "I don't know. Is it?"

"Hell no!" I said.

"You hit him."

"After he hit me . . . What about Malcolm Floyd? He's the one I'd have in here."

"Malcolm was playing poker in the Shiner bunkhouse with a half dozen men that night, and they played until it was almost time to catch horses. There's no way he could've done it."

"So, you just said, 'Hell, let's go get Concho—he mighta done it'?"

Jackson shook his head. "No . . . Five different people have told me they saw Sid hit you at the dance, and they said you hit him back. And at least that many said they heard what he said about you and his wife."

"Well, that wasn't true!" I said.

"It wasn't? I don't know how many people have told me about the way you and Mrs. Van were dancing together and smiling and looking into each other's eyes that night. They said it seemed like she was more with you than with Sid."

"We all came together."

"You know what I mean. And you say you were at Drippin' Springs all night the night Sid was killed, but nobody can verify that, can they?"

I looked at him but didn't say anything.

"Can they? If there is, tell me."

I didn't say anything.

"Then you tell me," Jackson said, "if you were me, who would you have brought in?"

"What about him killin' himself?" I asked.

"Why? Because you and his wife—"

"NO! I said that wasn't true!"

"But if he thought it was, then that might've made him kill himself? Is that what you're sayin'?"

"Well . . . yeah," I finally said. "I never would've thought it, but who knows what a man will do when he's drunk and feelin' sorry for himself."

Jackson smiled and shook his head. "The only guns we found in the whole rubble were burned up in the gun case. What'd he do—shoot himself through the heart and then put the gun up before he started the fire?"

"Why'd he have his boots on?" I asked.

"I don't know . . . you tell me. And why didn't Judith hear the shot that killed him? There's only two explanations for that—either Sid was killed somewhere else and his body brought back in the house without waking her or else she wasn't there like she said she was. Which do you think it was?"

I didn't say anything for a little bit, and then, "I'd like to talk to her."

"That'll be up to her . . . maybe you ought to talk to *me*. What happened that night, Concho? If she was in bed when the fire started, like she said, why did she have a dress on when we got there? Maybe she did fall asleep with it on—but if she took her wedding ring off when she was getting ready for bed, then why didn't she take the dress off? Maybe I'll have to bring her in, too."

"No! There's no way Judith could've done it."

"Why?"

"Judith kill Sid? If you think that, then you don't know her!"

"But you do? You . . . know her?"

"It's just all crazy, Denver," I said. "All of it!"

"Crazy? Yeah . . . damn right it is. Most of these kinds of deals are."

"You don't think I did it, do you? I mean, not really. But, since Sid was so well known, you had to bring *somebody* in, didn't you? And who better than me. Bring the stranger in and nobody will be upset and everybody will feel better. There's just one trouble with the whole deal, Denver—I'm not guilty."

"The way things look against you, Concho, if I hadn't brought you in, I wouldn't have been doing my job."

"Can Robert Shiner prove where *he* was that night?"

"I haven't asked him," Jackson said.

"Well, damn! I guess it slipped your mind."

"So far as I know, there's only two reasons men kill other men—money or women. Robert's already got both, and he's not goin' anywhere, anyway."

"How many rich men do you know who don't want more? Besides that, there was bad blood between Shiner and Sid. Hell, Shiner even threatened to have his men shoot any of Sid's cattle that got on his land."

"I'll present the evidence against you to the grand jury in the morning."

"What then?"

"Then either there'll be a trial or I'll let you go. I'll get you a plate of food from the cafe if you're hungry."

"Oh yeah. I've got a hell of an appetite," I said. "You can bet it's the thing weighin' heaviest on my mind right now."

"Suit yourself," Jackson said as he walked back into his office.

I was lying on the bunk in my cell a couple of hours later when I heard piano music.

Sid's funeral.

"Hey!" I said as I stood up and stepped to the bars. "I want to go to the funeral!"

Jackson stepped into the doorway with his hat on and his shirt collar buttoned. "I'd rather jump off Devil's Rim than walk into that church with you."

So I sat there alone and listened to "Rock of

Ages" and "When They Ring the Golden Bells" come floating into my cell from the Methodist church at the far end of Main Street. And then it got quiet.

I thought about Judith sitting in the front pew with Sid's coffin in front of her at the foot of the altar and wondered how she was doing and what she was thinking and what the preacher was saying and how could Sid be dead and me in jail for his murder.

After a while I heard them singing "Sweet By and By" and knew the service was over; they'd be going to the cemetery to put Sid's charred remains into a grave on the grassy bank of Chugwater Creek. I wondered who'd be standing beside Judith and how she'd take Sid's burial.

In my mind, I was still convinced that Sid had killed himself. In so doing, he had not only destroyed himself, but maybe me and Judith as well—which was probably exactly what he had in mind. That is, *if* he had anything in mind other than bitterness and revenge and whiskey.

When Jackson stepped back into the doorway a little while later, unbuttoning his collar and wiping the sweat off his forehead, I looked up and said, "How was it? Did Judith fall apart?"

Jackson nodded.

"A lot of people attend the funeral?"

" 'Bout everybody from town and the nearby

ranches. There were lots of whispers and stares at her. Everybody's heard about you and Judith. The preacher even said how unjust it was that a good man—a crippled man at that—should pay for the sins of others with his life. Then he talked about the fires of hell and how only Sid's body was burned, but the ones responsible would feel their souls burning in hell for eternity."

"And anybody sitting on that grand jury in the morning will probably have been sitting in that church today, right?"

"Yep," Jackson said.

"Well, hell," I said, looking down at the cell floor. "You might just as well hang me now and get it over with, hadn't you?"

"That's not the first time I've heard that today."

Shorty came in about sundown. He stopped in the doorway and said, "You ready to get out of this oven and go to Mexico now?"

I looked up at him. "I'm more than ready," I said. "How're things out at the ranch?"

"I 'bout got it back on a payin' basis. The last feller who was out there got things in a hell of a mess."

"You're tellin' me," I said.

"What do you want me to do?" he asked as he stepped inside the cell area and stopped across the bars from me.

"Either wake me up from this bad dream or get a case of dynamite."

"You know what I think?" Shorty said.

"What?"

"I think you've been set up."

"By who?"

"The way I see it, Mrs. Van's got her a good ranch with a ready buyer—and no crippled husband to make her miserable. Maybe her and that goddamn Shiner were in it together, or maybe—"

"I don't want to hear any more, Shorty! Judith wouldn't do that!"

"It's time you woke up, Concho—you've always been a naive bastard."

"You don't know what you're talking about."

"Have you told Jackson that you weren't alone that night at Drippin' Springs?"

I shook my head.

"Has she even been to see you?"

"The funeral was this afternoon," I said. "Besides, what would it look like if she did?"

"It's nice to see that there's two of you lookin' out for her benefit, but who's lookin' out for yours? You're the one in jail."

"You don't need to tell me that again."

"Nobody can tell you a damn thing, can they."

"Absolutely nothin'," I said.

"There's two kinds of men in this world, Concho . . ."

"Yeah—you're damn right there is!" I said. "And by god, I'm one of 'em!"

224

We looked at each other and before long we were laughing.

Sheriff Jackson stepped into the doorway and looked at us. "Nice to see you find my jail so entertainin'," he said.

"It ain't your jail," Shorty said, wiping his eyes with the back of a hand, "it's this dumb son of bitch here. I'll see you later, Concho. I'm gonna go get that dynamite."

"Dynamite?" Jackson said, coming closer to my cell.

"Yeah," Shorty said as he walked past the sheriff. "For Concho to put underneath his head . . . maybe it'll blow some sense into him."

"I don't know why in the hell I like ya'll," Jackson said.

"I don't know why you like me," Shorty said as he stopped in the doorway and turned toward us. "But hell, you gotta like Concho there. I mean . . . look at him—a poor, senseless creature—you either gotta like him or put him out of his misery."

"I'd just as soon you hadn't said that," I said.

"Do you know anything about this that you feel you ought to tell me, Shorty?" Jackson asked.

"Yeah, I sure as hell do," he said. And then walked on through the door and out of the office.

Somehow, not long after sundown, I dozed off on the bunk in the cell.

And what did I do? Even after all that had happened?

I dreamed. But not about Sid—how he might have died, or who might have killed him—or about the house burning to the ground or about me being brought in with my hands tied to the saddle horn and then locked in a cell.

No. None of that. Nothing that would make sense to dream about.

I dreamed about Judith.

Hazel eyes soft and happy, watching me with an easy smile as she slowly took her hair down in a room where only a single candle flickered behind her. I don't know where we were, but it felt like it was a thousand miles from anybody else and we had all the time in the world to do nothing but be with each other.

Then I woke up and heard singing.

Only this time the singing wasn't coming from the Methodist church at the end of Main Street, it was coming from the choir in the Basin Bar across the street and down the block: *"Come along boys, tell you a tale . . . of Concho Smith on the devil's trail. Now, Concho Smith, he wanted a wife . . . so he took Sid Van's and he took Sid's life."*

I heard Jackson loading a rifle, and pretty soon he stepped into the doorway and said, "I think I'd keep away from that window if I were you."

"What's going on?" I asked.

"Nothin' but a bunch of drunks acting like idiots over at the bar," he said. "Nothin' to worry about."

"Is that why you loaded that rifle?"

"I've been in this job long enough to not take anything for granted. But I'm not afraid of a bunch of drunks."

"You may not be," I said. "But I sure as hell am."

Jackson smiled. "Just stay away from the window," he said, and went back to his desk.

I lay back down on the bunk and a few minutes later heard someone knocking on the outside door. I raised my head and saw Jackson slide his chair back, step around his desk, and walk toward the door. I heard him raise the shade on the door. Then I heard him unlock it.

"Well . . . ," I heard him say, "I wondered . . ." He paused. "You ought to come in so we can close the door." Then I heard him shut the door, work the lock, and pull the shade back down. "Do you want to sit down?" After another pause he said, "All right, let's sit over there at the desk. Let me close this door."

As he walked to the door between the office and the cells I could see a woman standing behind him.

I stopped breathing, straining to see who it was.

In the instant before the door closed, I caught a glimpse of who he had let in the office. She was facing the desk and had her back toward the door that was closing. But it was her.

Judith.

I sat alone in my dark cell and looked at the lantern light coming underneath the door. Sometimes I could hear the singing from the bar, and every now and then I could hear Jackson's deep voice on the other side of the door, but never heard Judith's voice at all.

They talked for a long time. A long time.

I knew what they were talking about. Or did I?

Would Jackson let her talk to me? Or would she even ask?

"Mail-order bride, comin' to town . . . she married Sid Van and they settled down. Concho Smith, came one day . . . tasted her charms, now he'll have to pay."

The son of a bitches. And I didn't have to be told which son of a bitch was leading the singing.

"Concho Smith, once wild and free . . . will soon be swingin' from a hangin' tree."

Damn.

After an eternity—at least an hour—passed, the door opened and Jackson stood in it for a second, silhouetted against the lantern on the desk behind him.

When he stepped into the cell area I could see Judith sitting in the chair in front of his desk with her back still to the door.

"Judith told me," Jackson said.

"Told you . . . what?" I asked.

"About you and her. Why didn't you tell me?"

"What'd she say?" I said after a few seconds. "What'd she tell you?"

"That she went to Drippin' Springs that night to see you. That she drank some whiskey so she'd have the nerve. That she got dizzy and sick and couldn't. Is that right?"

"It wasn't just because of the whiskey that she couldn't," I said.

"She said she was there the rest of the night . . . asleep."

"Yeah. She wanted to go home as soon as she woke up. That's when we saw the smoke."

"You said it wasn't just because of the whiskey that she couldn't."

"It wasn't."

"Why else couldn't she?"

"Well . . . because of Sid, of course."

"So . . . you knew that night that no matter what, you'd never have her—not as long as Sid was around, huh?"

"No." I shook my head. "I never thought that. Well . . . I mean not actually."

"But you knew then that that's the way it was, didn't you?"

"Well . . . that's the way it *was*—the way it should've been."

"I'll bet you were disappointed, weren't you?"

"Yeah," I said. "I'll tell you the truth, Denver. Right or wrong, I guess I'm in love with her, but I know—and I knew then—that if she ever committed adultery it would destroy her along with whatever she felt for me."

"That sounds mighty noble of you," Jackson said.

"Oh, I wasn't noble. Didn't mean to sound like I was. If it hadn't been for Judith . . ."

"Or Sid?"

"What do you mean?"

Jackson shrugged. "You said if it hadn't been for Judith . . . but really it was Sid stopping both of you, wasn't it?"

"If you want to say it that way, I guess so."

"It doesn't matter how I say it," he said. "Only how the grand jury does."

"What? Hell, I thought . . . Judith told you where I was! Do you think she'd lie about something like that! Don't you know how hard it was for her to come tell you?"

"No, I don't think she'd lie about something like that. And I'm sure it was hard for her to come here. But it hasn't helped you a damn bit. If possible, it's even made it worse for you."

"What?"

Jackson looked me in the eye. "I'll be truthful with you, Concho—I don't think you did it, but . . ."

"But if you turn me loose you don't know who you'd bring in, do you. And since everyone else around here evidently thinks I did it . . . Well, what the hell, huh? Let's leave the stranger in jail even if we don't think he's guilty. I mean . . . hell! Sid's been killed and *somebody's* gotta be in jail!" I turned around and kicked the bars between my cell and the next one.

"I—and everybody else—suspected you and Judith were sweet on each other," Jackson said. "But until now that's all it was—suspicion and gossip. Now you both admit it's true, and there's your motive. You even said that as long as Sid was around, you knew you'd never have her."

I turned around and faced him with my hand out. "But I was with *her* all night! She just told you so!"

"No," he said, "that's not exactly what she said. She said that after she got sick she went to sleep and slept until morning. How can she say you were at the camp all that time? She can't. So there's your opportunity."

"What? I didn't leave! I paced the floor and rolled cigarettes for quite a while, and then I laid down on Shorty's bedroll and sleep awhile. I'd just been awake long enough to make a pot of coffee when Judith woke up."

"But of course, there's no way to prove that, is there. There was just you and Judith, and she was asleep. You were agitated and upset—maybe you just went down to talk to Sid and things got out of hand. Maybe he was still drunk and—"

231

"Go to hell," I said. "Go to goddamn hell! Your mind's made up and—"

"I've already told you that I don't really think you did it—you might have, but I don't think so. I'm just tellin' you how the grand jury may look at it in the morning."

"So much for tellin' the truth, huh? Judith threw her reputation away by coming here and being honest . . . she'd have been better off if she'd lied!"

"I don't know about her," Jackson said. "But you might have been better off if she'd kept the truth to herself."

I turned around again and faced the wall. There was singing coming from the bar again: *"Concho Smith wanted some fun . . . now it's time to pay for things he's done."*

Jackson sighed. "I don't know why in the hell I ever agreed to run again. I'd better walk Judith back to the hotel."

I turned around. "She's staying at the hotel?"

"Yeah—she said it got pretty uncomfortable staying at the Stiles'. Harry and Helen had known Sid a long time, you know. Judith is still kind of an outsider around here."

"Does she . . . did she . . . want to talk to me?"

"She didn't mention it."

CHAPTER 18

IT DIDN'T TAKE the grand jury long.

I'd thought I expected to be indicted, but from the way it hit me when Jackson told me I was, maybe I hadn't expected it after all. Or maybe it was the fact that the trial would be in only five days—on the Monday coming up—that hit so hard. Or maybe it was hearing Jackson say the words "indicted you for capital murder." Or maybe it was the fact that he also told me the territorial governor was sending a special prosecutor from Santa Fe to handle the case.

After I heard all of that I stepped back from the bars and sat down on the edge of the bunk, I guess looking every bit as downcast as I felt.

"Looks like something finally got your attention," Jackson said.

"It was got before," I said. "It sure is now."

"I wish there was something I knew to do," he said. "But hell, Concho, I'm just a cow-country sheriff. I don't know anything about investigatin' a murder like this."

"Then you still don't think I did it, do you?"

"I don't think so. But it *looks* like you did it. Maybe you've been set up."

I raised my head and looked at him. "By who?"

"Judith."

I put my head in my hands and laughed. "You must've been talking to Shorty."

"No . . . I haven't seen Shorty since he left here yesterday afternoon. Why? Does he think the same thing?"

"Yeah," I said as I raised my head again. "That oughta tell you how much sense that makes."

"She had more to gain than anybody by Sid's death. That ranch is hers now, and you said yourself that Robert Shiner's just dyin' to buy it. I talked to some people who heard Shiner's offer to Sid. At a fair-market price of five dollars an acre, that's seventy-five thousand dollars, not countin' what she'd get for the cattle and horses."

"That's crazy."

"I've been thinkin' about it—nobody can really prove where she was that night either. And don't say she was with you all the time, because you said you went to sleep on Shorty's bedroll. Maybe she wasn't drunk at all, and when you went to sleep she—"

"No . . . hell no," I said. "A mouse runnin' across the floor wakes me up, and besides I can tell when a horse has just been put up, and hers hadn't."

"Maybe she had a partner then."

"No!" I said.

"Well, I don't know," Jackson said. "I just know that her testimony is gonna kill you in court if she tells it like she told me. It seems honest, and she acts like she's really ashamed of what she did and is embarrassed to even tell it, but then when you think about it"—he shook his head—"it nails your hide to the wall."

"But everything she said is the truth."

"Yeah, and it sounds like it too. You know what really is gonna get you is the fact that you *knew* Sid was the reason she couldn't go through with it that night."

"Well, that's the truth, too."

"Did she tell you that?"

"Yeah."

"See—the more honest *she* is, the worse it makes *you* look."

About an hour later Robert Shiner and Malcolm Floyd walked into the sheriff's office. The door was open between the office and the cells, and I could hear everything that was said.

After they exchanged their hellos Shiner said, "I want to commend you on the way you didn't waste any time in bringing Smith in."

"Just doin' my job," Jackson said. "I just hope he's the right man."

"He is," Shiner said. "It couldn't have been anybody else. I knew he was a troublemaker the first time I saw him out at Smokey Hill. I never could figure why Sid hired a drifter like him to start with."

"Is that all you needed?" Jackson asked.

"No," Malcolm said. "We think something might've happened to Billy."

"Billy Wright?"

"Yeah," Malcolm said. "You know, me and him swapped places about a week ago—he went out to Clear Lake for a while and I went to headquarters."

"I didn't know that," Jackson said. "But okay—so, why do you think something's happened to him?"

"Because I can't find him," Malcolm said. "It doesn't look like he's been at Clear Lake for a couple of days. He hasn't been at headquarters, and none of the men in the other camps or nobody in town has seen him either."

"That's a pretty big ranch," Jackson said. "Maybe he's camped out somewhere."

"His bedroll is still at Clear Lake," Malcolm said. "And it's not but five or six miles from there to Sid's house. He'd have had to've seen the smoke when it burned, but he didn't come over there, did he?"

"No," Jackson said. "He wasn't there."

"He wasn't at the funeral either," Shiner said.

I stood up and walked to the cell door. What Malcolm was saying *was* sort of strange.

"His saddle's not there, a horse is gone, and nobody's seen him," Malcolm said again. "Seems like he disappeared the same time Concho killed Sid."

My god, I thought, *Billy's* the one who killed Sid and then left the country! His disappearance made sense that way.

"Maybe Concho killed Billy too," Malcolm said.

"Now, wait a minute!" Jackson said. "Why in the world would he do that?"

"Revenge," Malcolm said. "They'd already been in two fights since Concho's been here—and that's not countin' the night at the dance. They got into it at the wagon when Concho came over to get Sid's cattle—Concho blindsided him that time. And then a few days after that, me and Billy caught him trying to steal a Shiner calf and they got into it again. But when we left that time, Concho was the one lyin' on the ground and twitchin'."

I'd heard about all I could stand. "You son of a bitch!" I yelled. "If I'd been trottin' around shootin' people, you can bet I wouldn't have overlooked you!"

"Hear that?" Shiner said as Jackson got up from his chair and headed for the door between the cells and the office. "That was an out-and-out death threat if I ever heard—"

The door slammed shut, and from then on I couldn't make out what they were saying, but I knew it wasn't anything to do with what a fine fellow I was.

Before long, the door opened again and Jackson stepped into it with a red face.

"Looks like it'd be a good time to dig out all your old unsolved crimes," I said. "Missin' cats and dogs, cut fences, a bucket somebody tied on some old lady's milk cow . . . hell, I'm handy—blame it on me! Rapin', pillagin', plunderin', whatever you got, here I am."

"One time Sid told me that he didn't know about you," Jackson said.

"When'd he tell you that?"

"Oh, I just rode out to the ranch one day to get out of town for a while and see how he was doing. He said you and Judith were water-gappin'."

"What else did he say?"

"He said you had a way of bringin' out the most in people. I asked him if he meant the most good or the most bad, and he said he didn't know, not then anyway."

"What's that got to do with anything?" I asked.

"I don't know. Do you know anything about Billy Wright?"

"I know he didn't savvy nothin' about anything, and if you were punchin' cows with him you'd just as well plan on flankin' yourself up."

"And that's all?"

"That was enough for me."

When Jackson got to the doorway I said, "Has it ever occurred to you that it might not be a coincidence that nobody's seen him since Sid was killed?"

He stopped and turned around. "You mean other

than the fact that you might've killed 'em both just like Malcolm said."

"Yeah, other than that."

"Yeah, it has," he said, and shut the door between us.

Shorty came to the jail that afternoon, about two—maybe two and a half sheets—into the wind.

"I've been indicted for capital murder," I said, "but I don't want you worrying so much about it and gettin' all upset."

"I'm worried about you, all right," he slurred, "but I'm not upset—hell, I'm pretty damn relaxed."

"I can tell," I said.

"What you need is a good dose of old Sugar."

"What I need is a good dose of sagebrush and sunshine."

"Well, you can count on me, Concho—I can guaran-damn-tee you that! Hell . . . you say the word, and I'll put so much dynamite under this 'dobe cracker box it'll be scattered from here to Smokey Hill and from rim to rim."

"About two more drinks, and you won't even be able to find this 'dobe cracker box," I said.

"Hmmm . . . I'll find her. You ready to get out of this low-rent son a bitch right now? Hell, I'll—"

"No, I don't want you to do that," I said. "I'll tell you what you can do, though—you can scour around and see if you can find Billy Wright. Seems like he's among the missin'. Of course, Shiner and Malcolm told the sheriff I killed him too. Billy and Malcolm traded places, so you might prowl around the Clear Lake country to start with. It's strange he disappeared right when Sid got killed."

"Hell, he probably got off from the house and can't find his way back—especially if him and Malcolm ain't still joined at the hip. But, I'll take a look. If he's anywhere, I'll damn sure find him—you can count on that." He took three or four steps toward the far end of the cell area before he stopped and turned around and started walking toward the door.

"Maybe you oughta wait till mornin'," I said when he walked past me.

"Good idea," he said without stopping.

I was sitting on my bunk picking at the food on the plate Denver brought me from the cafe and trying to keep the sweat from dripping off my chin into it when I heard someone yell, "Denver! Come out here and take a look at this!" It was Malcolm's voice.

"What is it?" he yelled from his desk.

"Just come out here and look!"

I saw him get up from his desk and walk toward the door. I could tell from his bootsteps that he walked out onto the boardwalk.

I stood up and stood next to the bars with my ear turned toward the door.

"This is Billy's horse and saddle."

"You sure?" Jackson asked.

"Hell, yeah, I'm sure!"

"Where'd you find him?"

"I found him back out at Clear Lake on the outside of the horse pasture, walkin' the fence. From the way he's scratched up, I'd say he's been over a fence or two somewhere."

"But no sign of Billy, huh?"

"No, but come here and look—there's blood on the swells of his saddle. Better get some men together and start looking for him."

"I can't just go off like that—not with Concho in jail."

"I'll do it then," Malcolm said.

There was a pause. Then Jackson said, "All right—but you're not going to be wearin' a badge."

"I don't need a goddamn badge," Malcolm said. "I'm just afraid of what we're goin' to find—that son of a bitch in there killed Billy just like he killed Sid."

"Now wait a minute!" Jackson said. "We don't even know if Billy's dead. Hell, his horse could've fallen on him or bucked him off or anything."

"Could have," Malcolm said. "But you don't really think that any more than I do, do you?"

"I think we gotta wait till we find Billy before we know what to think."

"You just stay here and baby-sit," Malcolm said. "I'll get some men together and we'll start first thing in the morning. Billy's out there somewhere, and we'll damn sure find him."

I thought most of the men Malcolm would line up to look for Billy would come from the choir at the bar across the street. And I hoped they'd think they ought to get a good night's sleep so they'd be fresh and sharp the next morning.

But no such luck. Not long after dark, the singing began again and I laid on my bunk, stared at the ceiling, and listened to it.

The lantern wasn't lit in the cell area, but Jackson had the door to his office open, and yellow light from the lantern on his desk came through the open door. For some reason—I guess because of the singing and me thinking that I wished I didn't have anything more to worry about than making up words to some stupid song and drinking whiskey—I didn't hear him get up and open the outside door or hear him talking to anybody.

But then I saw a long shadow in the oblong pattern of light on the floor between the rows of cells and turned my head to see who was standing in the doorway. It was a short somebody, but too short even to be Shorty, and the hat he had on was a floppy kind of farmer hat.

When I saw the hat come off and the head shake and the hair fall down I stood up.

"Judith?"

"Sheriff Jackson didn't want me to come at all," she said. "But he said that if I insisted, I should dress like a man. He brought me the clothes this afternoon and said not to come till dark." She stood there silently for a little while and then said, "Do you even want to see me at all?"

"Yes," I said, moving to the bars of my cell and putting my hands on them. "I do."

She stopped just on the other side of the bars and looked at me with the lantern light shining on the side of her face. Those green eyes weren't dancing and sparkling, but she was beautiful nonetheless. For the life of me, I couldn't help but want to reach out and touch her.

"There's something I've got to ask you," I said. "You don't think for a minute that I'd ever do anything to Sid, do you?"

"I know you didn't shoot him or start the fire, Concho. I've never thought that." Then she smiled in a sad kind of way.

Judith turned her head and looked at Jackson, who was seated behind his desk. Then she looked back at me. "What are we going to do?" she asked. "A lot of people in the basin want to hang you right now, you know. They want to hang you and burn me at the stake, I guess."

"I don't know what we're going to do," I said. "Jackson doesn't think I did it, though."

"No . . . ," she said, "he thinks I set you up in some way. Did you know that?"

"Yeah, I know."

"You don't believe that, do you?"

"Of course I don't!" I said.

"Good."

"Can you think of *anybody* who might've had a reason to kill Sid?"

She shook her head. "I think he killed himself."

"Yeah . . . me too. But, like Jackson said, the jury is gonna convict *somebody* of doin' it."

"Sid had a lawyer friend in New Mexico. Socorro. I'll try to get him to defend you."

Jackson scooted his chair back and walked to the door. "I think you ought to be goin'," he said. "While the drunks are still in the bar."

She put her hand back on top of mine and looked at me. "I know we're equally guilty of what we've done," she said, "but it's not murder. Beyond that . . . I don't know anything, not anymore."

"Neither do I," I said.

"Mrs. Van . . . ?" Jackson said.

She stepped back and leaned over so her hair would fall in front of her. Then she put the hat over it and straightened up, looked at me once again, and walked out the door and toward the front of the office with Jackson beside her. "I don't think it would be a good idea for you to come back," I heard him say.

"I wish I could convince you that Concho's not . . ."

"It's not me you need to convince," he said. "It'll be that jury."

"But how can I do that and tell the truth? You've already said that—"

"Just be sure the truth is what you tell."

"And you don't think what I told you is the truth?"

I could hear the exasperation in his voice as he worked the lock on the door. "Be careful out there."

When he locked the front door again, he walked to the door to the cell area and stopped there. "If word was to get out that she came to see you, it would be like throwin' kerosene on a fire."

"I guess so," I said.

"I wonder if she knows that?"

"Of course she does," I said.

"But she came anyway, didn't she? . . . Maybe you ought to ask yourself why she'd do that."

"I know why she did it."

"Do you?" he asked, and then walked back to his desk.

Late in the afternoon of the next day, Malcolm yelled at Jackson from outside. When Jackson opened the door, I heard Malcolm say, "We didn't find hide nor hair of him, but we found that goddamn Shorty Wayman prowlin' around Clear Lake."

"Well, I guess he's got as much right to look as anybody else," Jackson said.

"He doesn't have any right to be out there for *any* reason!"

"I'd think you might want his help," Jackson said.

"Well, I don't! And he'd better not set foot on Shiner land again."

"I can't keep him from looking," Jackson said. "Besides, I've got enough to worry about right here."

"Then you take care of what's in here, and I'll take care of what's out there," Malcolm said. "What about your letting Judith in here last night dressed up like a man?"

Jackson said, "I don't answer to you, Malcolm."

"You'll have to answer to a lot of people next election," Malcolm said.

"Maybe . . . maybe not. But for now I sure as hell don't answer to you."

"What're they tryin' to pull? Did you listen to what they had to say, or did you leave 'em alone and stick your head in the sand? Did you search her before you let her in? And why'd you let her in at all, dressed like that? One of my friends is dead and another is missin', and you're just—"

"You didn't give a damn about Sid Van! And we

don't even know what happened to Billy—if anything has!"

"People are gettin' pretty upset about what's going on, Denver. You'd better take notice of that."

"What's goin' on is that Sid's been killed, I've arrested a man, he's been indicted, and the trial will be next Monday. You either try to find Billy or stay out at the ranch and play cowboy. Either way, I wish to hell you'd quit hangin' around the bar at night, singing those stupid songs that everybody in town can hear. You just remember what I said—you get out of line, and you'll be in one of these cells."

Then I heard the door slam and saw Jackson walk back to his desk, sit down, and put his head in his hands. I knew what he was feeling because I was feeling the same thing—the basin seemed to be taking in so much distrust and bitterness that you could almost feel the seams that held it all together stretching and stretching some more, a thread popping here and then another over there. You had to wonder—how much could those seams hold before the whole thing came apart? The only thing that seemed to be holding was Judith's and my constant faith in each other.

Shorty came to the jail just before dark to tell me that he hadn't had any luck in finding Billy. He said he ran into Malcolm and six other men, most of them Shiner cowboys that he knew, and that Malcolm had threatened him if he ever saw him on Shiner land again. He said he told Malcolm what he could do with his threats. He said he got to the Clear Lake camp before Malcolm did and that Billy's bedroll and shaving mug and razor and what looked like most of his clothes were still there. It looked like Billy just rode off one day and hadn't come back yet.

After he told me that, Shorty sat down on the floor and leaned against the bars on the cell opposite mine without saying anything for a while.

"What're you thinkin'?" I said. "It's not like you to be so quiet."

"I don't know"—he wiped his lips on the back of his hand—"but have you thought that maybe Billy and Judith are in this together? Could be they'd been seeing each other and nobody else knew about it, and—"

"Oh, I see," I said. "He killed Sid, set the house afire, cut his hand a little with his knife, dropped some blood on the swells of his saddle, and boogered his horse."

"Aren't you going to ask why he cut his hand and boogered his horse instead of just trottin' back to Clear Lake?"

"Absolutely not," I said.

"Then I'll tell you anyway. Oh, by the way"— he pointed his finger at me—"keep in mind that

Billy and Malcolm swapped places just a few days before this happened. Billy had to get someplace where he'd be alone. If you're stayin' in the bunkhouse at headquarters you can't just saddle a horse and trot off by yourself without somebody knowin' it—at least by the next mornin'—which leaves you with having to explain where you went and what you did when someone's been killed sometime before daylight that very same mornin'."

I stood up and stepped to the barred window of my cell and looked outside at the trash barrels behind the jail.

"Billy had to go to Clear Lake," Shorty continued, "so he could leave there anytime he wanted to and no one would ever know it. After Billy kills Sid and does the blood and boogerin' deal he leaves the country on another horse and saddle that he's stashed somewhere close by. Nobody's gonna suspect him of killin' Sid because it doesn't look like he just left the country—it's like something terrible's happened to him too. After the poor Mrs. Van mourns Sid a few respectable months, she sells the ranch to Robert Shiner and goes off to meet Billy."

I looked out the window and didn't say anything. And when I still didn't say anything, Shorty said, "Aren't you goin' to say anything?"

"Yeah," I said.

"What?"

"If Denver don't light that trash barrel, the cats and skunks are gonna play hell with it."

"I'm goin' to the bar," Shorty said.

"That'll be real smart, with Malcolm and his crew over there," I said.

I didn't turn around, but I heard Shorty get up and say to Sheriff Jackson as he walked out, "Did you ever try to drive an old cow through a gate that was wide open, but when you got her up to it she'd just trot on past it? And then you'd bring her back and she'd trot past it again? Or you'd hold her up right in front of it and she'd look right at it and then come back over the top of you? It was just like she could see every little old thing except for that ten-foot gate, and then she was just blind as a bat."

CHAPTER 19

THE NEXT DAY the prosecutor from Sante Fe and reporters from newspapers in Socorro, Santa Fe, Omaha, El Paso, and maybe a few others that Denver forgot to tell me about showed up.

Denver wouldn't let any of the reporters talk to me, but I guess they nearly hounded him and Judith and Shorty to death. Denver said they talked to everybody who was in the posse that brought me in, and of course, Malcolm was an invaluable source of information for them. Apparently they were more than a little delighted with the free entertainment provided nightly at the Basin Bar—made "great copy," or so they told Denver. Denver said there was no danger of the telegraph operator losing his job for lack of anything to do as long as they were in town.

In order to accommodate all the spectators expected at the trial, it was decided it would be held in the big new barn that Grady Vinson had built but hadn't yet stocked with lumber. I could see how that would be handy for all those testifying about the events of the night of the dance.

The prosecutor who had been sent from Santa Fe was a nice enough man in his midthirties, wearing wire-rimmed glasses and a city suit and named Boyd Rentfro.

The morning before the trial, Jackson introduced me to the lawyer Judith had hired for me. His name was Dexter Crawford. He looked so young and innocent that I bet if you said boo to him he'd come unglued right in front of your eyes. Somehow, those weren't the qualities I was hoping he would have.

"Don't you think you should've been here a couple of days ago?" I asked.

"Well, actually I'm not the attorney Mrs. Van requested," Crawford said as if he were apologizing for spilling his milk at the dinner table. "That would have been Buck McGregor. But, being a friend of the victim, he didn't think he could defend you. We had a vote whether to send anybody at all—the vote was in the affirmative. I'm here now, and I'll try to give you adequate counsel. I'm a junior partner in the firm."

I looked at him and smiled but didn't say anything.

"Now tell me what happened," Dexter said.

He took a few notes while I was talking, and when I was finished he closed his notebook.

"What do you think?" I asked.

"Think?"

"Yeah . . . you know, about how it looks. Isn't all of it what you call 'circumstancial evidence'?"

"I . . . huh . . . yes . . . I believe it is," he said.

We looked at each other for a minute, and then he said, "Well . . . I guess I should get checked into the hotel."

"Yeah . . . I'll bet you should," I agreed. "I'll bet you're grimy as hell, aren't you?"

"Oh, I really am!" he said.

"I appreciate your stopping by," I said.

"Why . . . I appreciate your help—I really do, Mr. Smith!"

"Shoot," I said. "A feller tryin' to give me adequate counsel? The least I can do is help."

"Holy shit . . . ," I muttered to myself as Dexter tipped his narrow-brimmed hat to Jackson on his way out. "Where's that dynamite?"

A couple of minutes later, Shorty came in and

said, "Who was that kid I bumped into when I was comin' in here?"

"That's my adequate counsel," I said. "Name's Dexter."

"Where'd he come from?"

"Socorro . . . Judith hired him for me. Well, actually, he's not the one she wanted."

"Uh-huh," Shorty said. "Scared yet?"

"Yeah."

And I was. Suddenly, I could picture Vinson's barn filled to the rafters with spectators and at the far end of it a . . . a stage. And on that stage was a desk with a chair behind it for the judge and another chair sitting by itself in front where Judith would sit all alone in front of hundreds of eyes and tell what happened the night she came to Dripping Springs as the judge tried to keep order over all the whooping and the hollering. It would be hell for her.

Or would it? I didn't want it to happen, but—although I tried chinking it up as best I could—I could feel my faith in Judith beginning to crumble. If she got up there and told the truth, I was probably a dead man. I'd pictured both of us being noble throughout all of this, keeping on the high road and holding to the truth. But now, with the trial less than twenty-four hours away, the low road seemed a much less undesirable place upon which to break dust than it once had, and if I could just find a way to get on it, I was sure I could trot right down the middle of it with no qualms at all—the truth didn't seem nearly as important as it had a couple of days ago. I decided, in fact, that the ability to lie and be damn good at it suddenly seemed to be a trait well worth fostering. It was scary how quick all of that changed in my mind, and not something in which I took a great deal of pride. But neither could I see much pride—and even less future—in hanging for something I didn't do.

All Judith would have to do was to get up there and say she'd lied when she said she'd gone to sleep right after we'd gone inside the cabin at Dripping Springs—lied because she was ashamed to admit what we were really doing. And we did it right up until the time we saw the smoke.

Would the jury believe her? Hell, they might! That would soil both of our reputations for sure— but then again, even without that, our reputations weren't exactly going to be hot-water fresh and sunshine-dried by the time the trial was over. Besides, right then the soiled reputation of a drifting live cowboy seemed head-and-shoulders above any reputation a drifting dead cowboy might have—no matter how bravely, or otherwise, said cowboy had climbed the gallows. I'd much rather the people of Chugwater Basin talked about what a scoundrel that Concho Smith was than how well he had died.

"I need to talk to Judith," I told Shorty.

"She went back out to the ranch yesterday afternoon to get away from the reporters," he said. "I stayed in her hotel room and she stayed at Dripping Springs."

I hated myself for the thought that suddenly entered my head. "Maybe you should've—"

"Gone back out there last night to see if she met anybody?"

"Yeah," I reluctantly said with an embarrassed nod.

"I did. All night. Nobody came and she never left—but at least you're gettin' your head on straight now."

"I still need to talk to her," I said.

"All right," Shorty said. "I'll go back out there and get her right now."

After Shorty left the jail, I paced my cell from end to end and from side to side, over and over again. I had no appetite for the plate of food Jackson brought from the cafe and slid underneath my cell door. I felt like a cull bull in a narrow chute at a packing plant, waiting to walk onto the kill floor.

In the middle of the afternoon Shorty returned.

"I couldn't find her," he said.

"What do you mean you couldn't find her?" I asked.

"I mean she wasn't there—not at Drippin' Springs, not around the barn, not anywhere. I thought maybe I'd missed her somewhere and she'd come back to town, but she's not in her room and the hotel clerk said he hadn't seen her."

"Well, damn, Shorty . . . I need to talk to her!"

"Well, damn, Concho . . . I can't find her!"

I rubbed my forehead and looked at Jackson standing in the doorway between the cells and the office.

"I'm gonna go get drunk," Shorty said.

"Yeah . . . hell, yeah," I said. "Go get drunk, that'd be the thing to do, all right!"

"Glad to see we agree on something," he said as he walked past Jackson.

"Damn!" I said, clenching my teeth as Jackson went back to his desk. "Damn! Damn! Damn!"

There I was, perfectly willing to travel the low road and no way to get on it.

It was a little bit after dark when I heard a loud knock—actually, more like a banging—on the front door.

I stopped my pacing and saw Jackson walk toward the door carrying his rifle. He asked who it was.

"An acquaintance of Concho Smith's!" Shorty slurred loudly.

Jackson mumbled something, then I heard him unlock and open the door.

"Well, come on. You can see Concho after you give me the bottle."

"It's for my acquaintance in there," Shorty said.

"No . . . prisoners aren't allowed to have liquor."

"Well then . . . to hell with you. I'll just go see old Sugar at the bar."

"No . . . come on—you're not goin' anywhere for the rest of the night. You can sleep it off in the cell next to Concho's."

I heard the front door being shut and locked, and then Jackson said, "Let me put this rifle down and help you."

"Thank you, Den—Den—Denver," Shorty said. "From now on, I think I'll be your friend instead of Concho's. Hell, you're an upstandin' citizen in the 'munity and more worthy of a friend of my cal—caliber. Wouldn't you say?"

"Whatever you say, Shorty," Jackson said as they came into view through the doorway. Jackson had put Shorty's arm over his neck, and although Shorty was trying to walk, by the time they came through the doorway Jackson was all but dragging him.

"You're not gonna put me in here with the riffraff, are you?" Shorty asked.

"Good god," I said as Jackson leaned him against the bars so he could unlock the cell next to mine.

"Good god to you too," Shorty said. "I had a damn fine repu—repu—reputation before I started hangin' around the Van ranch."

As Denver struggled to get Shorty's limber form

into the cell, the sheriff said, "I'm gonna . . . put you on this bun . . ."

And then just like—that!—Sheriff Jackson was out on his feet.

Shorty's uppercut had traveled only a few inches, but he was stout as an ox and his fists were hard as rocks and carried the wallop of a mule's hoof behind them. I knew because I'd felt them before, myself.

I was stunned, taken as completely by surprise as Jackson had been. The only difference was, I wasn't sliding down jailhouse bars with my eyes rolled back in the top of my head.

"Sorry about that, Denver," Shorty said as Jackson came to a stop in a sitting position with his chin resting on his chest. "Close your mouth, Concho . . . you didn't really think I'd get drunk at a time like this, did you?"

"Of course I did," I said as he scooped up the ring that had the big cell key on it off the floor. "Are you sure you know what you're doin'?"

"How in the hell am I supposed to?" he said as he unlocked my cell. "Let's find something to tie Denver up with and gag hi—"

There was a knock on the front door—three short raps.

Shorty and I froze and looked at each other.

Three more raps, this time a little louder, came from the door in the office.

"Shit!" he whispered.

"Sheriff Jackson?" a voice from the other side of the door said in a loud whisper.

"Damn . . . ," I whispered. "It's Judith!"

"Maybe she'll go away," Shorty said.

Judith knocked again, still louder than before. "Sheriff Jackson! It's Judith Van . . . Please let me in!"

"I'll see if I can get rid of her before she attracts attention," Shorty said in a disgusted voice.

I followed him to the door between the cells and the office and watched while he blew out the lantern on Jackson's desk and hurried to the front door.

"Sheriff Jackson?" Judith said again, this time rattling the doorknob.

"Judith!" Shorty whispered toward the door.

"Yes?" she answered. "Shorty?"

"Yeah."

"Let me in," she said. "Is something wrong? Where's Sheriff Jackson?"

"He's here," Shorty said. "Nothing's wrong."

"Why did the lantern go out?"

"Because it did! Jackson said you'd have to come back later—early in the mornin'."

"No!" she said in a voice that was hardly a whisper. "Let me in now! I need to talk to Concho!"

There was barely enough light in the office for us to see each other, but through that dim light Shorty looked at me and saw me shake my head.

"He doesn't want to see you," Shorty said.

"Well, he's going to or I'll stay right here and pound on this door all night! Let me talk to Sheriff Jackson!"

"Damn, Judith!" Shorty said.

"I mean it!"

"Are you by yourself?" he asked.

"Well . . . yes!"

Shorty worked the lock and cracked the door only wide enough for Judith to slip into the office. Then he quickly shut the door, locked it, and picked up the rifle that Jackson had leaned on the wall next to the door when he'd let Shorty in. "I thought you said you were alone!" he said.

"I am!"

"Then who's that out in the street?"

"Well . . . most of them are reporters," she said. "But they're not *with* me! What's . . . ?" Then she saw me—or saw a figure—standing in the other doorway. "Sheriff Jackson . . . ?" she said in an unsure voice.

"No," I whispered, "it's me."

"Concho?" she said.

"Shhh!" Shorty said.

"What are you doing?" she asked, taking a couple of steps toward me and trying to bring her voice back to a whisper.

"What 'n the hell do you think we're doin'!" Shorty said.

"Where's Sheriff Jackson?" she asked.

"He's okay," I said. "I promise he's not hurt."

"Don't do this, Concho," she said.

"Where were you today?" Shorty asked.

"Where was I? I was out at the ranch all day."

"It doesn't matter now, anyway," I said.

"I couldn't find you out there," Shorty said. "And I looked everywhere."

"I was on top of Big Butte Mesa."

"Yeah?" Shorty said. "With who?"

"I was up there alone . . . thinking."

"Well, I could've used a little company!" I said. "You know, it's not much fun being in a jail cell by yourself the day before you think you're gonna get sentenced to hang for something you didn't do!"

She took two more steps toward me and stopped just in front of me. "I'm sorry," she said, "but I was trying to think of what to do. Didn't the lawyer from Socorro come to see you?"

I laughed. "Yeah—some kid lawyer came. Did you really think the head of the law firm and a good friend of Sid's would come defend me—or even send someone he thought would give me a fighting chance?"

"I didn't know they were friends!" she said. "I just knew he'd done some work for Sid before. I didn't know anybody else!"

"We can't stand here and talk all night," Shorty said. "Judith, you've gotta decide right now . . . are you in this with us, or not?"

"In *this?* Escaping! . . . I don't know . . . I wanted to talk to you about the trial—maybe we shouldn't—"

"You either help us," Shorty said, "or you hang Concho . . ."

She paused, then let out a long, nervous breath. "I don't know. What is it you want me to do?"

"All you've got to do," Shorty said, "is to walk out of here like nothing's wrong and make sure all those damn reporters follow you. In the mornin', you can say what you want to . . . but if I was you, I'd say everything was fine when you were here—that you talked to Concho and Sheriff Jackson a few minutes and then left."

She looked at me. "Concho . . . are you sure this is what you want to do?"

"On the other hand," Shorty said, "how do we know we can trust you? How do we know that you won't spill your guts as soon as you get outside?"

"We don't have any choice," I said. "There isn't a back door, and it's gonna be mighty hard to slip past a bunch of newspaper reporters standin' a few feet away with their eyes glued to the door. Judith, all I can say is you should do whatever you think you have to do just like I am."

"Where will you go?" she asked.

"Mexico," I said. "With luck we could cross the Rio Grande tomorrow night."

"Will I ever see you again?" she asked nervously, holding her hands together.

"Do you want to, after all of this?"

"Yes," she whispered after a moment.

And then suddenly she had her arms around me, hugging me tight. She lifted her face toward mine and kissed me on the lips with every bit as much feeling as she had the night in the draw—the night I should have left the basin for good.

"Be careful," she whispered. "Please, be careful."

"I will . . . Will you be okay?"

"Yes. Will you find some way to let me know where you are?"

"I'll think of something," I said. "But it'll be a while."

"Come on, you two," Shorty said impatiently. "Good god! That's what started this whole mess!"

Judith stepped back, turned around, and walked toward the door while Shorty unlocked it. Just before he opened the door for her, Judith stopped. "I know what you think of me, Shorty," she said. "But you're wrong . . . and I'll prove it."

"I hope you do," he said as he opened the door for her and stood behind it.

As soon as Shorty closed the door behind Judith, we heard, "Mrs. Van! Mrs. Van!" from the reporters.

Then we heard the last thing in the world we wanted to hear, Judith saying, "Malcolm!"

CHAPTER 20

LIFE IS A strange thing.

I never expected to find myself breaking out in a sweat while trying to escape from jail in the dark of night hearing a clickety-click-click as Shorty Wayman cocked a thirty-thirty.

"Damn!" I whispered, wishing I were anywhere else in the world but right there. Then I experienced a sudden feeling of relief—the whole thing was so impossible that I knew I had to be dreaming. All I had to do was to force myself to wake up and I'd see bright stars overhead and smell the coffee that the cook was boiling. That bedroll I'd be in on the hard ground was never going to feel so good, and I wouldn't care if I had to ride the most owl-headed, counterfeit, spoiled horse in the whole remuda that morning—in fact, I was looking damn forward to it. Kick me, tangle me up, buck me off on a prickly pear flat a hundred miles from the wagon—I was looking forward to every blessed moment of it.

But there was no waking from this nightmare. The sweat running down my back was real, just like the man on the other side of the door and Shorty gripping that cocked thirty-thirty were.

"At least you didn't sneak in there dressed like a man this time," Malcolm said to Judith. "What's going on in there?"

"Nothing," Judith answered in a surprisingly calm voice. "Sheriff Jackson just wanted to talk to me for a few minutes before the trial."

"In the dark? Hey, Den . . . !"

Judith laughed. "He said people were going to be banging on his door pretty soon if he didn't get that new wick in the lantern and get it lit again."

I tiptoed to the desk, struck a match on the sole of my boot, and lit the lantern while Shorty gently held the bottom of the window shade against the door.

"There . . . ," Judith said. "Finally!"

"Mrs. Van! Mrs. Van!" the reporters called to her.

"I'll talk to you in the lobby of the hotel!" Judith said loudly. Then softer: "I hate to ask you, Malcolm, but would you mind walking with me to the hotel and sitting with me until all these reporters leave? Having someone I know with me would mean a lot to me—unless you've turned on me like everyone else has."

I heard Malcolm reply, "I haven't turned on you, Judith. I'll be glad to walk you to the hotel—after I talk to Denver."

Shorty looked at me. I could read the cuss word he had on his tongue but held behind clenched teeth.

Jackson moaned, just loud enough so we could barely hear him.

Shorty hurried through the door leading to the cells while I tiptoed around the desk to the front door.

"Can't you talk to him later?" Judith asked.

Shorty brought Sheriff Jackson through the door from the cells much like Jackson had taken Shorty into the cells a few minutes ago—with an arm around his neck, more or less carrying him, but now Jackson's eyes were open.

"It'll just take a second," Malcolm said outside. "And then I'll go with you . . . and stay as long as you need me." I heard the barroom tone of his voice and wanted to jerk the door open and slap him. Then he banged on the door. "Denver!" he yelled. "Open the door a minute!"

"Thank you," I heard Judith whisper. "But let's go right now. The sooner we get rid of these reporters the sooner we can talk in private . . . If you'd like to do that?"

Shorty had put Jackson in the chair and was dipping his fingers in a glass of water on the desk and flipping it into Jackson's face while Jackson opened and closed his eyes and turned his head back and forth.

"Yeah," Malcolm said. "Yeah, I'd *really* like that . . . as soon as I see Denver." He banged on the door again and twisted the doorknob. "Denver!"

Jackson was sitting up straighter in the chair and rubbing his face with his hands.

"It must be more important for you to see Sheriff Jackson than it is to be with me!" Judith said. "This has not been an easy time for me, Malcolm, and . . . oh, well, forget it—I'll go to the hotel and face the reporters by myself. *Don't* bother coming over later."

"No . . . wait," Malcolm said, "just one second! . . . Denver!"

Shorty leaned over and whispered something to Jackson, who squeezed his eyes shut, opened them again, and nodded. "What do you want, Malcolm?" Jackson called out.

"Denver? Is that you?"

Shorty whispered to Jackson again.

"Who do you think it is?" Jackson said in a louder, firmer voice.

"Is everything okay in there?" Malcolm asked.

Jackson turned his head and looked up at Shorty, who raised his eyebrows and nodded.

"Yeah!" Jackson yelled.

"See!" Judith said. "Can we go now?"

After a few silent seconds, Malcom said, "Yeah . . . let's go."

We heard Judith and Malcolm's footsteps on the boardwalk and then it grew silent outside.

Shorty looked at me and let out a sigh of relief.

"That bastard . . . ," I said softly, picturing him walking across the street to the hotel beside Judith and knowing what was on his mind.

"I'm sorry about this, Denver," Shorty said.

"After the street clears, we'll just tie you up and gag you and be on our way. We won't take you with us."

"Thanks," he said. "I'm sure as hell not up to an all-night ride. You don't mind if I pull up my britches and look at my leg, do you?" Denver asked. "I think you must've skinned it."

"You don't have a gun in your boot top, do you?" I asked.

He laughed in a used-up way. "Yeah . . . sure I do. You see how suspicious you get of everything as soon as you start down that owl-hoot trail? Are you sure this is what you want to do?"

"It's a long ways from what I *want* to do," I said as I watched him lean over and pull up his right britches leg. "But—what was it Rentfro said? The die is cast."

"Yeah . . . I know what you mean," he said as he looked at his leg and rubbed it. "Damn, it's sore from right there all the way down past the top of my boot. Must be this damn little gun rubbin' on it."

Then he stood up with that "damn little gun" in his hand, the hammer pulled back and his finger on the trigger. The gun wasn't even big enough to have its own trigger guard, but it was at least thirty caliber and had a cylinder big enough to hold at least five shells. And the "damn little gun" was pointed right at Shorty.

"Shit!" Shorty said as he stepped back slowly

and lowered the rifle's muzzle until it was pointing at Jackson. "What in the hell else can happen!"

"Put your gun down," Jackson said to Shorty.

"You won't use that thing!" Shorty said. But his voice wasn't brimming over with confidence, and you could hear the question he didn't ask: "Will you?"

"The thing is . . . ," Jackson said, "I will. And maybe you will, too. But, if I do, I'll just be an old man tryin' to do his job. What will you be?"

The only sound I heard in that office for the next little while was my heart pounding in my head, a wagon rattling down the street, and a town dog barking.

Then there were two loud footsteps on the boardwalk and an even louder knock on the door.

"Denver!" a man's voice I didn't recognize yelled.

"This is gettin' goddamn ridiculous!" Shorty whispered.

"Denver!" the man yelled again as he tried the knob.

"Baldy?" Jackson yelled. "Is that you?"

"Hell, yes, it's me! You ain't gonna believe who just rode bareback into town!"

"Billy Wright?" Jackson replied loudly.

"No . . . hell no! It was Sid!"

Me and Shorty looked at each other.

"Who?!" Jackson yelled.

"You heard me—Sid Van!"

"Have you been at the bar all night, Baldy?" Jackson yelled.

"Hell, no!"

"How could Sid have rode into town!"

"I don't know! You think you're surprised?! Hell, I was the first one who seen him! I helped carry 'im to Doc Hammons—he's in there right now! Come on, dammit! Come on over there!" And then there were steps on the boardwalk again, followed by silence.

We all three spent the next few seconds looking at each other. Finally, Jackson said, "Don't you boys think you ought to call this whole thing off till we find out what in the hell's going on?"

"It's a trick, Malcolm's idea of a joke."

"Maybe," Jackson agreed, "but it looks like even he'd have more sense than to make something like *that* up! What if it's true and you don't find out till you're in Mexico and you've got jail-break charges against you?"

I thought awhile, and then I said "Damn!" and turned around and started walking to the door leading back to the cells.

"Where you goin'?" Shorty asked.

"Back to that goddamn cell!" I said.

"What about me?" he asked.

"Well, hell—you're the one smart enough to plan this elaborate-assed jailbreak, surely you can figure *something* out," I said. "There wasn't no way in hell you were ever goin' to shoot Denver anyway, and you know it."

I stopped at the door and turned around and looked at him.

"Well, hell," Shorty said, letting the hammer down easy and then handing the rifle to Jackson. "Take the goddamn thing and give me the goddamn cell keys so I can lock the goddamn prisoner up! And then I want you to lock me up, Denver, and don't you *dare* even *think* about lettin' me out till this whole thing is settled once and for all."

Denver took the rifle and looked at me and then at Shorty. Finally, he just shook his head, and a trace of a smile flitted across his lips as he said, "Do y'all have any idea what you did with the keys?"

I started pacing the floor of my cell the minute Sheriff Jackson locked it and went out the front door. Shorty just stretched out on the bunk in his cell with his hat over his face and told me to pace as quietly as I could.

It was at least an hour before Jackson came back with a strange look on his face.

"Well?" I asked. "Who was it? Or was it anybody at all?"

"It was Sid," Jackson said.

I sat down on the edge of my bunk. "How? I mean . . ."

"That was Billy Wright we buried in Sid's grave," Jackson said.

271

"Well . . . what in the hell happened . . . and where's Sid been?"

"It's not all sorted out yet," he said as he put the key in the lock on my cell door, turned it, and pulled the door open. "But you're both free to go."

"What about the . . . jailbreak?" I asked as Jackson unlocked Shorty's cell door.

"As far as I'm concerned it never happened—and if you say it did, I'll say you're lyin'," he said as he stepped back so Shorty could walk out. "I'm damn sick and tired of havin' you two around here. If I ever have to come after you again I'll be shootin' on sight! Now get out—I'm closin' this establishment for the night and going to bed. Oh yeah . . . Judith is waitin' for you at Doc Hammons's office."

CHAPTER 21

TWO HOURS EARLIER I'd thought the next time I walked out the door of a sheriff's office I'd be in shackles and there'd be people standing shoulder to shoulder to watch me walk to Grady Vinson's new barn, where'd I'd be put on trial for my life. An hour and fifty minutes ago I had been broken out of my cell and was trying to figure out some way to sneak out the door without being seen. Now, I was walking out into the warm night a free man.

Horse water and manure never smelled so sweet on warm air.

"I'll go around to the back and get our horses," Shorty said.

"I'll meet you over at Doc Hammons's," I told him as I looked across the street and to the left at the doctor's office.

There were a handful of men standing around in the street in front. When they saw me coming, they stopped talking and stared. When I got to within a few feet of the house they slowly began stepping back so I could pass through.

Judith was standing on the boardwalk in front of Dr. Hammons's door. She looked at me with tired eyes, but she forced a smile on her lips and stepped off the boardwalk to give me a quick hug. "Thank god you're okay," she whispered in my ear and then stepped quickly back.

"I can't believe this—where has he been?" I asked.

"I don't know, but he wants to see us . . . together."

"How does he look?" I asked.

"I haven't seen him yet," she said. "Sheriff Jackson just said Sid wanted to see us at the same time."

As soon as Judith knocked on the door, Dr. Hammons opened it and stepped back to let us in. "Right through that door," he said, looking toward a door on the other side of the room.

"How is he?" I asked.

"He's been through a lot, but he's going to be all right," he said.

Judith opened the door and we stepped inside a small room lighted by a small lantern on a table beside a bed. There was hardly anything else in the room.

Sid was lying on the bed with a sheet over him. He had two pillows under his head and was wearing an undershirt.

I took my hat off and closed the door, trying to get used to the idea that he wasn't dead.

He wasn't shaved, but his hair was washed and combed. He might have looked a little thinner than he had been, and his face was sunburned, but other than that he looked fine to me.

Judith seemed unsure of herself, like she didn't know what she was supposed to do or say. She stepped to the side of the bed, touched his arm, and in a voice I could just barely hear said, "Hello, Sid."

I was standing at the foot of the bed. I didn't say anything and neither did he. He just lay there and looked at us for a while in the dim lantern light.

Finally, he did speak. He said, "You look tired, Judith." His voice was a little weak, but even taking that into consideration it still sounded different.

"We thought you were dead," she said.

"I know," he said. "I nearly was. I didn't know if I'd ever see you again."

He cast his eyes down at me. "Denver said they were about to put you on trial for killing me."

"Yeah," I said.

"It's a good thing for you that I got here when I did, wasn't it?" he said.

"Yeah . . . I guess you could say that," I said.

"How do you feel?" Judith asked him.

"Oh, I'm a little weak and tired and pretty sore, but I'm a lot better off than I thought I'd be."

"What happened, Sid?" Judith finally asked. "What started the fire and why was Billy Wright in the house? Where have you been? What happened to you?"

"Sometime not long before daylight that morning," Sid said in a calm voice, looking at Judith, "I heard someone banging on the front door. I didn't get up. I was still pretty drunk. But he—it was Billy Wright—came in anyway. I sat up on the couch. At first I thought he was looking to start something, make trouble because I clobbered him with my crutch during that fight outside the dance. But I think he was drunk, too—I don't know. I remember him smiling. He asked if I knew where my wife was."

I glanced over at Judith. She had closed her eyes.

"I told him you were in bed. He called me a drunk fool, then said he knew where you were and it wasn't in bed—at least not the bed I thought you were in." Judith lowered her head. Sid went

275

on, "That got me so mad I picked up one of my crutches off the floor beside the couch and stood up and swung it at him. I called him a liar and told him to get the hell out. He caught the end of the crutch and held it for a few seconds, then shoved it back toward me and laughed. I staggered backward and fell on the floor next to the whiskey cabinet. Judith, you know that gun I kept in the little drawer in the bottom of the cabinet—well, I got it out. I wasn't going to shoot him, but I was tired of people thinking I wasn't a man anymore, of thinking they could just walk all over me.

"When he saw the gun he laughed again and started coming toward me. I thought when he got close enough I'd hit him, but when I swung at him he caught my hand, just like he'd caught the crutch. We struggled . . . and the gun went off. I didn't even know that I'd cocked it. But Billy fell backward with a hole in his heart and a look on his face that I'll never forget. I knew he was dead even before he hit the floor. He fell on top of the coffee table where the lantern was, and burning kerosene started running across the floor.

"My crutches were behind the fire, so I had to make it back to your room without them. I had to get you out . . . but you weren't there. I looked everywhere and yelled for you . . . but you weren't anywhere.

"I went back up the hall to where Billy was and the fire had already spread all across the front of the room. It was everywhere but the picture window on the north wall. I tried to walk to it but fell down, so I crawled to it and pulled myself up and pushed against it with my shoulder until it broke and I fell through it onto the ground.

"I wasn't thinking very straight. I was still drunk and . . . everything that had happened. All I could think of was making you pay, Judith—you too, Concho. As I lay there beside the house, watching it go up in flames, I thought of a way to hurt you both, to make you feel guilty. I decided to hide and make you think something terrible had happened to me like it had Billy. I guess right then, it never dawned on me that Billy would be burned so bad that everybody would think the body was mine. All I could think about was making you worry and wonder and fret and blame yourself. I planned to hide for most of the day, and then I'd say that I'd just gone off in a daze. Then I'd ask you where you were when the fire started and tell you that if you'd been there we could have saved the house.

"I crawled to Billy's horse, got on him somehow, and rode in the opposite direction of Dripping Springs—because I knew that's where you were. By then it was just starting to get light.

"I'd cut my belly on the window when I fell out of the house, but I didn't even know it till I'd ridden a mile or so. But it didn't matter. Nothing mattered. I rode Billy's horse all the way to a big salt-cedar thicket on Chugwater Creek just across the creek from Devil's Trail. It was hot and my shirt was soaked with blood and sweat, but I was chilled.

"I hadn't had anything but whiskey since noon the day before, and I could feel it starting to want to come back up. I had to get off and lie down, and I did right there in the brush with the flies and the gnats swarming over me.

"The next thing I knew, it was almost dark, Billy's horse was gone and I couldn't stop shaking. I was sick and nobody knew where I was—maybe they didn't even know I was still alive—and I didn't have my crutches.

"When I came to again, the sun was beating down on me—I guessed it was the next day, but I wasn't sure. I wasn't shaking quite as bad as I had been, but I had spots in front of my eyes and I needed a drink. I crawled through the salt-cedar bushes to the edge of the creek and drank enough warm, thick alkali water to make me sick again.

"I curled up on the hot sand right there across the creek from Devil's Rim. I knew that if I stayed there like that, I'd die slow and miserable and my carcass would dry up like an old cow's does. I thought a man shouldn't have to die like an old cow lying at a water hole. If I'd had the gun with me I would've just killed myself, but then something happened. I won't say I heard a small voice or that I heard a voice at all, but suddenly *something* seemed to say to me that I could stay right there and die or I could try to live. You know, Judith, I used to think I'd rather be dead than crippled. But I pushed myself up to my knees. I knew that Parker Springs was about two miles due south across a rocky flat full of prickly pear. I crawled along the creek bank until I finally found two dead cottonwood branches that I could use as crutches, and then I started across that flat. I didn't even think about going all the way. I thought, I'll just go as far as I can. At least, out there on the flat somebody might see me.

"But nobody saw me. The rough ends of those cottonwood branches ate my armpits up. I think it took a day and a half, but somehow I made it all the way. The only thing that kept me alive was sucking the juice from around the seeds in the prickly pear. I got my hands and lips and tongue full of little splinters, but I made it. I couldn't believe it! I'd made it all the way to Parker Springs. I drank water and ate plums from a thicket and lay in the shade for a few hours and slept.

"When I woke up, I knew I had another long walk—at least four miles—to home, and I dreaded it, but now I thought I could do it. I *knew* I could do it! So, I filled my pockets with plums and started out again.

"It took another couple of days to get to the house. At least, all the way back to where the house *used* to be. I got there right before dark and managed to whistle the horses up and get one caught and bridled. I climbed up on the fence and, after three or four tries, finally got on and came to town."

"Sid . . . ," Judith said, touching his arm again, "I'm sorry about . . ."

Sid smiled and held his hand up to stop her. "Don't," he said, shaking his head.

"I'm so glad you're safe," Judith said. "But a lot has happened, Sid. There's a lot of talk about me and Concho."

"And I won't believe a word of it . . . not now," Sid said. "I know what kind of woman you are— if you were going to cheat on me you'd have done it long before now." Now Sid shifted his gaze to me. "And I know you too—you're hardheaded but you're not the kind of man to take advantage of a crippled man. I need you around here—I hope you're going to stay. I'll try to hire some men to go out and start building our house back."

I didn't know what to say, so I just looked at him.

"Y'all don't need to stay here," Sid said. "I've got to get some rest anyway. You can take me back out to the ranch tomorrow after I talk to Denver some more, Judith. There'll be a grand jury about Billy's death—but I'll face whatever comes. Y'all go on now."

"I'll stay here for a while," Judith said without looking at me.

Sid looked at me and smiled again. "Thanks for everything you've done for us, Concho."

"Sure." I put my hat on and walked out the door, across the office, and back into the warm air that smelled of horse water and manure. Shorty was sitting on his horse, holding Drifter's reins.

I had no doubt about things happening with Billy exactly the way Sid said, or that he had nearly died. But I did not believe the part about him trusting Judith and being thankful to me. But if Judith wanted to believe it, that was up to her. I was fed up with everybody and everything in the whole basin.

"How is he?" Shorty asked as he handed me Drifter's reins.

"Full of bullshit as a Christmas turkey," I said.

We were about two doors down from the Basin Bar on our way out of town when drunken singing came through the swinging doors out into the dark street: *"Come along boys, tell you a tale . . . of Concho Smith on the Devil's Trail."*

"Sounds like Malcolm's havin' a good time again," Shorty said.

I pulled Drifter to a stop in front of the bar, handed his reins to Shorty, and stepped up on the boardwalk in front of the swinging doors.

"Concho Smith's ridin' again . . . lookin' for . . . ," Malcolm was singing as I stepped through the doors. The singing stopped. He was leaning

against the bar between a couple of bar girls. The bartender was the only other person in the bar.

I took one of the leather straps that held the outer doors shut in front of the swinging doors. I closed it with a knot.

"What in the sam hill are you doin'?" the bartender yelled.

"You're closin' early tonight," I said.

"Like hell I . . ."

"Get out," I said.

Malcolm laughed. The bartender reached under the bar and pulled out an ax handle.

"He prefers cedar stays," Malcolm said.

The bartender came around the end of the bar with the ax handle. "Now get . . ." He looked past me and said with a laugh, "Denver, this son of a bitch thinks he can just come in here and close the doors!"

"I think that's a good idea," Sheriff Denver Jackson said behind me.

"Hell . . . he can't . . . !"

"No, but, I can," Jackson said. "You're closed, Nathan. Now, you and both you girls get out."

The bartender raised the ax handle, and I heard Jackson cock both barrels of the shotgun he was holding. "I mean it!" he said.

The bartender looked at Jackson, then at me, and finally tossed the ax handle to Malcolm and walked out with the girls.

The details of what me and Malcolm engaged in

over the next few minutes aren't important. I won't say that I was unbloodied, only unbowed. And when the chandelier overhead was finally the only thing moving in the bar, I was the one standing with the ax handle and Malcolm was the one curled up on the floor with broken ribs.

"Enough!" he said.

"I'll be the one decidin' that," I said as I turned the ax handle and used the flat part to spank his butt.

Then I dragged him to the swinging doors, picked him up, and heaved him through, breaking the windows in both and leaving one hanging cockeyed on one hinge. When I stepped outside, Malcolm was lying on the boardwalk, moaning. Jackson and Robert Shiner were looking at him.

"I think that belongs to you, Little Bob," I said.

"Do something, Denver!" Shiner said.

"Like what?" Jackson asked.

"Arrest him and charge him with assault and destruction of property! You haven't forgot that I'm the one who owns this bar, have you?"

"No," Jackson said, "I haven't forgotten." Then he took his badge off and threw it on the ground next to Shiner's feet and said, "I'll tell you what, Robert, if you want him arrested, then you go ahead and do it yourself—I'm goin' to the house."

After I'd got back in the saddle, and above Robert Shiner's yelling and cussing, Jackson looked at me and Shorty and said, "I know you boys don't ever do what anybody tells you, but if I was you, I'd get the hell out of here."

When me and Shorty were riding out of Chugwater for the last time, he said, "You ever been in a country before where the only one who likes you is the sheriff?"

"Oh yeah," I said. "Lots of times."

CHAPTER 22

SHORTY HAD ROLLED our blankets, tied them on our packhorses before he'd ridden to town to "break me out of jail," and had tethered the horses inside the barn at the ranch. When we got back there it must have been close to midnight, and we decided to wait till daylight to leave. Shorty went right to sleep, but I didn't.

I could tell I'd never go to sleep so I decided to saddle Drifter again and make the short ride to Dripping Springs one last time. I could wash away the stale smell of the Chugwater jail in the cool water there and make a fresh pot of coffee in the cabin.

I'd been in the water for only a couple of minutes when Drifter threw his head up, looked toward the cabin, and nickered. My first thought was that it was Malcolm Floyd, and I couldn't believe that I was stupid enough to've come up here unarmed, especially after all that had happened.

Then from around the corner of the cabin a figure in a long skirt, leading a horse came into view and stopped midway between the darkened cabin and the pool of springwater.

Drifter snorted loudly, and for a few seconds even the insects and night birds seemed to fall silent as Judith and I looked at each other in the pale moonlight. Then, suddenly, the whole of the basin—from the north rim, to the tall tops of Smokey Hill and Big Butte Mesa and the bottoms of the creeks and washes clear to the south rim and all the furred and feathered creatures who dwelt between the two tall rims—seemed full of life.

The rest of that sweet night was ours and ours alone. But I knew even then, even as the waning moon slowly descended toward Smokey Hill, and as all drifting men come to learn sooner or later, such rare moments are not free.

Judith and I rode off the bench just as day was beginning to break. When we got back down to the barn, Shorty already had his bed rolled and was tying it on his packhorse.

He looked up at us and nodded but said nothing.

"Good-bye, Shorty," Judith said softly as she reined her horse away. "Take care of Concho."

Shorty watched her ride away for a few seconds and then went back to tying his bedroll on his packsaddle. "Was she cryin'?" he asked as he pulled the rope tight.

"I don't know," I answered.

"What's she going to do?"

"She's catching the train this morning, going back to Minnesota. Said she's had all of this basin and Sid she can stand. He didn't fool her any more than he did me."

A few minutes later all of my worldly possessions other than my saddle and the clothes I was wearing were tied onto Feather's back again.

Me and Shorty didn't say another word until we'd ridden to the top of the south rim of the basin. We stopped to let the horses blow and to reset our saddles.

When we were back in our saddles and leaning over our saddle horns looking down on the basin for the last time, Shorty said, "Reckon Sid can make it alone?"

"He won't be alone," I said. "He's got the devil for company—for some men that's enough, I guess."

"Would you have traded places with him? I mean, if you could've had his ranch and his horses and cattle—and Judith—in exchange for some son of a bitchin' horse fallin' on you and ruinin' your legs, would you have done it?"

"I don't know," I said honestly.

I heard a distant whistle blow and looked toward the east and saw the smoke of the train Judith would be taking. I knew the sharp, sudden pang of loneliness cutting through me was only the first installment of the debt owed on last night.

"You're thinkin' about her right now, aren't you?" Shorty asked.

"Naw," I said as I reined Drifter away from the rim and struck a trot toward the south. "Come on, we should've been in Mexico thirty days ago."

"Hell," Shorty said when he trotted up beside me, "what's thirty days to . . . ?" He caught himself and stopped.

I leaned over the saddle horn and looked at him. "You mean . . . to men like us?"

"Yeah," he said.

I thought a few seconds before I answered. Then I said, "Absolutely nothin'."

Shorty grinned. "You should be more like me," he said.

"If I was more like you I wouldn't be able to reach my stirrups," I said.

"You know what I mean," he said. "Here you are all long-faced and heartbroken over a woman. Now me—hell, I'm not gonna spend two minutes thinkin' about ol' Sugar."

After we'd trotted another couple of hundred yards, and without looking at him, I said, "I can understand that."

Shorty started laughing. Mexico lay ahead of us, and the train in the basin blew its whistle again behind us.

Center Point Publishing

600 Brooks Road ● PO Box 1
Thorndike ME 04986-0001 USA

(207) 568-3717

US & Canada:
1 800 929-9108
www.centerpointlargeprint.com